ONE TO PROTECT

By Tia Louise

One to Protect
Copyright © Tia Louise, 2014
www.facebook.com/AuthorTiaLouise
Printed in the United States of America.

Cover design by Jasmine Green
Jasminegreen.net

To the protectors and the lovers.

To Mr. TL.

Most of all to the readers who wanted more.

CONTENTS

CHAPTER 1: A SMALL SYMBOL
MELISSA

A cold blast of air steals my breath as I dash through the concrete parking garage, and I remember why I chose my cozy beach cottage in Wilmington over life in the city — even over life in a town the size of Princeton.

The doorman guarding the entrance is another reason.

Hired staff knowing all my moves, my comings and goings, who I'm expecting… It's a type of *déjà vu* that's way too close to my old life in Sloan's house, for comfort.

But Walter is nothing like Widlow or Hal, the housekeeper and driver who were basically paid spies in my ex-husband's Baltimore mansion. Walt stands just inside the glass doors in his maroon uniform waiting, and I see the moment recognition crosses his face. Jumping to open the door quickly, he greets me with a warm smile.

"Miss Jones!" His gloved hand covers the handle of my overnight bag as his other arm sweeps away the grocery sack I'm carrying. "Mr. Alexander didn't say you were coming. Let me help you."

His gravelly voice and doting personality remind me of an elderly relative.

My voice is smooth and high in contrast. "Derek doesn't *know* I'm coming. It's a surprise." I give his shoulder a squeeze, and a whiff of peppermint touches my nose. "I've asked you to call me Melissa."

With a wink, he turns and leads me to the elevator, where he presses the button. I study his salt-and-pepper grays peeking out from under his cap, thinking how perfect he is at his job. "I won't breathe a word about seeing you, then, and management would fire me on the spot if I called you by your first name."

"Ridiculous."

The doors open and he hesitates. "This is a pretty heavy load. Want me to call one of the boys to carry it up for you?"

"I carried it all the way to the front door by myself, no problem."

My eyes are wide, and a chuckle scrapes from his throat. "He's going to be so glad you're here. You're just what he needs."

"I heard it's been a tough week." We're holding up the elevator, but I'm curious if Nikki, Derek's office manager, might have exaggerated the situation.

The building has less than twenty residents, most of whom work the same crazy hours as my fiancé, so I'm pretty certain we're safe for a moment's chat.

"I wouldn't know, but I haven't seen him smile since Sunday."

"Thank God it's Friday then?"

He grins and touches his hat. "Yes, ma'am."

The doors close, and I lean back against the shiny metal walls, thinking about what I know. Late yesterday afternoon, I got a text from Nikki saying if there was any chance I could get away, *Mr. Alexander could use a friendly face. And a hug. Preferably using your thighs.*

I laugh and roll my eyes. Nikki and I have grown close since my second visit to the Alexander-Knight offices. On my first, I only had one thing on my mind, and it wasn't making friends. So much has changed since that day in November.

Now I get regular text updates from her, and her solution to most of her boss's problems is sleeping with me. Frequently. She usually complains he's impossible by the end of our weeks apart, but this time has been different. This time her message sounded worried instead of playful.

The elevator opens at the top floor of the complex, and I walk the short hall to his door. It's almost like living in a hotel, but inside, the condos are huge — only four to a level. Unlocking Derek's, I take a quick survey of the very male space. Leather couch, dark wood furnishings, enormous flat-screen television — make that *gigantic* flat-screen television. I think he said it's 110 inches?

The kitchen is granite and stainless and untouched. The entire condo is spotless. A service comes once a week to clean and do laundry, and his suits are picked up and delivered by the dry cleaner. I smile and shake my head. He probably never even sees the people who take care of him. It's all done by invisible elves as far as he's concerned. He just pays the bills. It's not a home — at least not the kind of loving home I plan to give him once we're finally together in the same city.

Setting the brown bag on the counter, I place one item in the refrigerator, the other in the freezer. I carefully selected both to remind him of a happy night, a night that started in a family restroom. A tingle fills my stomach at that white-hot memory.

Back to the present, I head straight to the master suite. My overnight case is on the dresser, and I quickly remove the few outfits I've brought for the weekend and place them in the top drawer reserved for my things. Then I pull out my toiletries bag and hit the bathroom.

It's only six, and he's not expecting me. No telling when he'll be here, but I want to freshen up after the eight-hour drive. It never gets shorter. We have *got* to get in the same location soon.

The bathroom is smooth beige stone on both the floors and countertops. The shower is matching tile, and is large and recessed like a cave, so there's no need for a door. I shove off my jeans and step in, switching on the dual showerheads while carefully avoiding the blast.

Back out, I lift my long, dark waves up and twist them into a knot then unbutton my white blouse and slide it off my shoulders. His little gold, floating heart sits right at the base of my throat. It wasn't an expensive gift, but when I touch it, my body floods with warmth remembering how he gave it to me. *His heart…*

Turning to the side in my matching red-lace bra and panties, my hands spread over my midsection. Still not showing, but my waist is definitely thicker as are my thighs. I've gone up a pant size, and I'm uncomfortable in everything I own besides loose dresses. This baby bump has got to pop out at some point so I can switch to maternity wear and stop looking like a marshmallow.

Underclothes off, I return to the shower-cave, moving under the spray with my head tilted back. It's hot, but not unbearably so, and the massaging motion of the jets soothes all the stress of the long drive away. I wash my face, turn and scrub the scented gel I brought all over myself, taking it easy on my breasts, which are tender these days.

I stand and allow the lovely hot water to envelop me like a soothing blanket. It feels so good after being out in the frigid evening air. Several minutes pass, and I finally shut it off, step out, and catch the towel hanging on the hook.

Quickly rubbing it over my legs and up my stomach, I pause when I reach my face and clutch it to my nose. His fresh, woodsy scent is all over the soft terry, and I inhale deeply. My eyes close as a wave of desire sweeps from my head, past my sensitive nipples, to the growing heat between my thighs. We spent an amazing Valentine's Day weekend together just five days ago, but I can't wait to see him again. The weeks apart are so lonely, even with friends around.

His robe is hanging on the back of the door. It also smells like him, though he rarely wears it. I pull it around me, leaving the belt untied. It's like an oversized dress on my small frame, and the scent combined with the silky fabric whispering across my private parts piques my longing for him even more.

Only one lamp lights the dim condo as I cross back to the kitchen for a bottle of water. The furniture is bare of any accessories or pictures — I've noted it before — but today something's new. A single wooden frame has appeared on the mantle since my last visit. Picking it up, I recognize the shot of us sitting on the beach. He's behind me, and my head is tilted to the side as he kisses the base of my neck. I love this picture. My best friend Elaine took it a few weeks ago, and I'd sent it to him. I hug the small symbol to my chest, thinking how his place is less the sterile fortress now. He has proof, a loving reminder of my place in his world.

———

Going to the enormous glass windows to look out and wait, only a few lights dot the downtown area. It's either too early or too wintery for most people to be out. With the tip of my finger, I touch the cold glass and try to imagine where he is right now. How much longer he'll work. When he'll be here with me…

A noise from the doorway, and I look over my shoulder. My chest squeezes when I see him enter. His heavy grey overcoat makes him look even taller than six-two, his shoulders broader. His dark hair is longer than usual, and it just touches his collar in gentle waves.

Vibration hums under my skin as I watch him silently, my fingers curl with longing to touch him.

He shrugs off the topcoat and hooks it on the rack, and I almost sigh audibly when I recognize the suit he's wearing. It's the same one from all those months ago when I would gaze at him on my laptop screen. Back then I only had my memories and my hands. Now I have the real thing, and it's perfect.

He doesn't see me, doesn't even know I'm here, and it takes all my strength not to call out to him. I'm waiting, wanting him to see me first. The entry light is on, and the stack of mail in his hand occupies his attention. His brow is lined, and even his shoulders appear tense. The combined effect reminds me of the very first night I saw him — so focused and controlled, so intense and intimidating. Giving in to him was so hot.

Touching my lips with my tongue, I long to peel that suit off him, leave it lying in a pile on the floor as I cover his skin with kisses, massaging his stress away. I remember the band holding up my hair and quickly pull it out. Long, dark waves sweep over my shoulders at the exact moment he looks up. Blue eyes meet mine, and my stomach tightens.

My arm drops, parting the robe, revealing a peek at my nude body underneath, and his confusion turns instantly to desire. Without a word, he tosses the mail on the table and shrugs out of his suit coat. He crosses the dining area fast. I can barely breathe as he gets closer, removing more clothing with each step. Tie off, fingers unfastening buttons, he's in front of me, shirt open, undershirt the only thing between his skin and mine.

Neither of us speaks. It's very possible I'll come the moment we touch, but I snatch the edge of the thin white tank and push it up his lined torso. Pressing my lips against his heated flesh, I slip my tongue out to taste him. Large hands go inside the robe to my bare skin, sliding down and gripping my ass.

A little gasp comes from my throat when he lifts me. I'm off my feet, weightless in his arms. My back is against the cold glass, and his light sprinkling of chest hair teases my nipples.

His mouth roughly covers mine, consuming the noises rising in my throat, and his waist is between my thighs, pressing my most sensitive areas. Firm lips part mine, and his tongue explores my mouth. His kisses are insistent and ravenous, and every time his hips push against my clit, flames of desire shimmer down my legs.

Gripping his broad shoulders, my fingers dig into his flesh pulling him closer as his mouth blazes a trail to my breasts. Soft lips followed by the scruff of his beard teases my skin, and I can't help a moan as my head drops back against the window.

"Oh, god," I gasp as he catches a straining nipple in his mouth and gives it a hard pull. The sensation registers directly to my core. I need him inside me now.

My hands are in his hair, pulling, threading the soft, dark locks, as his kisses climb back up my neck. He pulls little bits of my skin between his teeth as he goes, and his scent is all around me, intoxicating me.

"Now, baby. I need you now." I can't take much more of this or I'll combust. My thighs are already trembling, my inner muscles aching.

I feel him reposition, holding me with one arm as his other works below his waist. Breathless, I fumble to push his shirt further off his shoulders, wishing it would tear. I kiss his skin again; a hint of salt is on my tongue. In one movement, he boosts me up then sinks deep inside.

He lets out a deep groan, and I gasp. The size of him, his incredible fullness stretching me, is always a delicious greeting after being apart. I'm riding on that delicious edge, and by his next, hard thrust my orgasm roars through me.

"Ohh, god," I cry, gripping his shoulders, rocking my hips as best as I can against him.

His breathing is labored. Another thrust, and I'm pulling him closer, unable to get enough. My cries seem to make him move faster, and I clutch his shoulders as he rocks me.

"Deeper," I beg against his neck, my lips just touching his skin. He shudders and grants my request, and a second orgasm begins, hot and low in my stomach.

Powerful waves ripple up my body, and my muscles tighten. It's like electricity, flashing all the way to my scalp, leaving me momentarily blinded. Inside, I'm gripping and pulling him, until with a loud groan, he comes.

His hips jam into me hard, pushing me against the glass, and his hands tighten on my ass, pulling me flush against him. It's a mild pain mixed with the most incredible pleasure, and I never want it to stop.

We push and hold, grind and feel, until gradually our bodies calm, our movements become still. Spent, I drop my forehead against his neck, holding him through the last sparkling waves of pleasure. He's inside me, one arm tight around my waist, the other under my butt. Warm lips touch my head, and I'm in heaven.

As if waking from a dream, I lift my eyes, sliding my hands to his cheeks. At the sight of blue, love bursts inside me. Sometimes it's still hard for me to believe this beautiful man is mine.

"Hi." My voice is soft.

Fine lines pierce his temples in the most attractive way as he smiles back. "You're here." His deep voice massages my insides, and I can't resist kissing those cheeks, his eyes, the tip of his nose, his full lips. They part, and our tongues greet each other again.

Movement stirs below, inside me, and I lean back to meet his loving gaze. "I've been waiting for you to get here."

"If I'd known you were waiting, I'd have left two hours ago."

I laugh, kissing him and whispering, "I love you."

"I love you more." His arms tighten around me. "What made you decide to drive in? Not that I'm complaining."

"I heard you might need a visit."

His brow creases as he considers my meaning. "Patrick?"

Shaking my head, I peck his cheek again. "Nikki."

With that he exhales, dropping his forehead against my shoulder with a groan-laugh.

"What?" I laugh, too, at his exaggerated frustration. "She's not as bad as you make her out to be."

He lifts me and slides out. Standing in front of him, I wrap the robe around my waist as he adjusts and fastens his pants. Then he scoops me to him again, kissing my nose. "For this surprise, I'll get her a little gift."

"Oh! Speaking of surprises, come with me." Pulling him to the couch, I push him around and make him sit. "Sit here, and don't move. I mean it."

He grins, watching me leaning over him. The robe drifts apart, and of course, he catches my nipple between his fingers, giving it a small pinch. "Ow—stop!" I yelp a laugh. "I said don't move."

"Darlin', I haven' seen you in a week." He tries to grab me, but I dodge.

"Don't pull that southern charm on me."

"I'll pull more than that on you." The devilish twinkle in his eye almost causes me to forget my little surprise.

I manage to resist. "Just wait."

A quick pit-stop in the toilet to freshen up, and I dash to the kitchen. Opening the freezer, I pull out the bottle of cava I brought. Tiny bits of ice float in it, but I pop the cork and pour him a flute—ginger ale for me. Next I take the two large olive-salad sandwiches from the fridge and arrange them on plates. It's all loaded onto a tray, which I carry on my shoulder to the living room where he's waiting.

"What have you done?" His voice is full of warmth as he watches me from the sofa.

"Since you've been working too hard—"

"Exaggeration."

"Since you've been working too hard," I repeat, "I decided to recreate our relaxing spa vacation in the desert."

Placing the tray on the coffee table, I hand him his flute and lift mine. "To family restrooms."

He laughs and clinks back. "To the gorgeous woman who drives me to crazy extremes."

We sip and I crawl forward on the couch to kiss him and tell him again. "I love you."

He leans forward, placing his flute, the tray, my flute, all of it on the coffee table. Then his hands move through the open robe to pull me onto his lap in a straddle, facing him. Just that fast, his mouth is on my neck, nibbling and kissing. My eyes are closed, and I'm powerless.

"I love you more," he says beside my ear with a deep inhale. "You smell so good."

Threading my fingers in his hair, I kiss his temple. "I wore the red lace…"

A rumble of approval, and his lips touch that spot behind my ear, a light scruff against my skin, sending shivers flying down my legs.

"My favorite." His voice is thick as I pull his cheeks, reuniting our mouths.

For a moment, we make out like teenagers, hot and breathless, tongues entwining. He holds me against his bare chest, my elbows are bent, and my palms are on his cheeks. His mouth is like some rich, decadent chocolate I can never get enough of tasting. As we kiss, I feel him relax, and my hands slide behind his neck, my lips travel up to his brow. He hugs me against his torso and doesn't move. Neither do I.

This big, strong man saved me twice. If comfort is what he needs, I'm here to give it to him. I'm here to give him anything. After a few more breaths, his arms relax. I lean back and study his face a moment. The robe has dropped around my shoulders, so I'm basically sitting nude on his lap, but I don't care.

"Hungry?" I reach for the sandwich plate and hold it between us, right at our chins. "You probably won't think it's as good as Central Grocery, but I think it's delicious."

His blue eyes take me in before he bites. "Mmm…" is all I get.

Giggling, I lean forward and take a bite myself. The tangy, savory flavor of olives and smoky provolone fills my mouth.

"Delicious!" My voice is muffled.

His smile glows as he watches me, his voice full of love. "How's the baby?"

Lowering the sandwich to the plate, I turn and put it on the side table again. "I can't feel a thing, but the doctor said he's doing great."

My last checkup was a week ago, and we both agreed unless something unusual occurred, Derek could miss the routine exams. So far everything has been by the book.

"So he's a boy now?" I love his grin at the prospect of a little son.

Shrugging, I acquiesce. "Maybe... it's too soon to know."

His attention moves from my face to my abdomen. Large hands span my bare stomach before he leans forward and kisses me right below my sternum, right at the top of my belly.

"I love you," he whispers to the little bean growing there.

I'm certain my heart melts in that instant, and I catch his face again to cover it with kisses. He's right with me, lifting me in his arms and carrying me to the master suite. A California king-sized bed fills the space, and he spreads me out on the soft mattress, lying on his side next to me.

I trail my fingers lightly over his brow, to his temple, following a line to his strong jaw. He looks at me like I'm the most fragile thing in his bed—another detail he knows isn't true.

We don't disturb the moment, though. The truth might be that both of us are strong as iron, tough as flint, but holding each other, we know how precious it is that we're here, together.

The randomness of chance keeps us both in awe, and for that, we treasure these moments. After working so hard, our reunions are the sweetest bliss. He holds me, and I feel very needed and extremely sexy. This man is like water in the desert to me, and it isn't hard to see the feeling is mutual.

"I'm sorry I interrupted dinner." Leaning forward, he nibbles the skin at my neck, and a surge rises between my legs. "Can you wait?"

My voice is thick as I answer. "I guess so…"

His mouth moves to my stomach then lower. My heartbeat quickens, knowing what's coming. A kiss to my navel, his tongue lightly traces the small circle, and I whimper.

"You guess so?" The sly grin in his voice tells me he knows I'll wait. I'm buzzing with anticipation as it is.

One quick slide, one quick lift, and my thighs are open. Toes curled, I let out a little cry as soft lips, scratchy beard, trace a line down my inner thigh to the center where his warm tongue makes a slow pass around my clit.

"Oh, god!" I curl up, threading my fingers in the sides of his hair. "Derek!"

Blue eyes are on me in a grin as another hot, firm circle covers that sensitive bud hidden between the folds. I collapse back with a groan of pleasure.

He sucks and pulls as I writhe, covering my eyes as the pleasure roars through my pelvis. My hips follow the movements of his mouth. He doesn't stop, doesn't let up until I'm bucking and moaning, holding his head and trembling.

Two thick fingers push inside, and my knees rise on their own. One more little pull, and he kisses my stomach, on the way up before thrusting into me, rocking hard and fast.

He's the one groaning now, and I'm holding on, burning in my afterglow as he joins me, his second orgasm even stronger than the first. One large hand grips my ass, and the other is pressed against the wall behind me as he thrusts again and again, harder and deeper, before letting go with a low moan.

For a moment, he's still. I'm lying back on the bed, admiring his lined stomach and broad shoulders. His head drops, and I reach for him. With a swift scoop, he rolls us both to the side, and I'm clutched close against his chest, his arms around my waist. His lips press against my shoulder, and I try to remember what we were even saying before on the couch.

He exhales, speaking into my hair. "You have no idea how happy I am to see you."

That makes me laugh, and I squeeze him tighter. "I think you've shown me twice now."

"I intend to show you several more times before Sunday. I might not let you leave this bed." His tone sends a thrill to my stomach... which is followed by a loud rumble. We both laugh.

"Baby is not amused. You'd better run get our dinner before he starves."

He's up in a flash, pausing to lean back and kiss my forehead roughly before heading to the living room. I admire his tight rear view flexing as he walks out the door to our abandoned dinner. Then he's back, still sporting a semi along with the tray of food and drinks.

My head is shaking. "You're insatiable."

"And you're gorgeous."

"Flattery will get you everywhere." I fluff the pillows and sit back against them while he arranges the tray between us on the mattress.

A quick sip, and he puts the flute on the side table. "I feel bad having cava without you."

"Mmm, I don't mind. It reminds me of the night we met."

"You were the most amazing creature I'd ever seen, sitting at the bar, wrinkling that little nose with every sip." He touches my nose with a grin. "Adorable."

"That drink was disgusting. Seven and seven." I shudder and take another bite of sandwich. "This is much better."

"I was done for the moment I saw you. I couldn't stay away."

Nodding, I swallow my bite. "You were pretty intimidating being so focused, but lucky for you, I wasn't backing down anymore. From anything."

He doesn't speak, instead he traces a line down the side of my face, along my hairline as his lips tighten.

"Or I should say lucky for us," I continue. "Looking back, it was pretty reckless, actually. You could've been anybody." My eyes roam over his darkened expression, and I put my plate aside. "What are you thinking?"

"I had no idea what you were facing." A note of anger is in the background of his tone. "What was waiting for you at home."

My fingers lace with his, lowering his hand to my lap. "We've discussed this. That's all over now. It's the past. There's no point letting it ruin our present."

Being here with him, contemplating our life together, makes it more than easy to forget my old scars. Those are days I can easily let fade into the deep background.

"I know." He pulls me to him, and I curl into his chest. Showered, stomach full, sexually blissed out, my eyes start to drift.

He might be the one needing comfort, but in this moment, in his strong arms, I'm feeling as safe as a queen—and as sleepy as an expectant mother.

Derek's arms are tight around me, and his lips press a gentle kiss to the top of my head. It's the last thing I remember before drifting into happy slumber.

CHAPTER 2: SPECIAL SKILLS
DEREK

Only two hours have passed since I told Melissa goodbye, and already that tightness is creeping across my chest. It's a mixture of anger and needing her in my sight where I know she's safe.

She didn't press the subject, but all weekend I could tell she wanted to know what I was working on, what was "bothering me."

Damn Nikki. If I weren't so pleased by the luscious surprise of finding Mel waiting for me half-nude in my condo Friday night, I'd reprimand her for keeping tabs on me. I don't need an office manager who doubles as my mother, or who reports my behavior back to my aunt — or my fiancée.

Melissa stayed to this morning, Monday. She's so different than when we first met. Even back then she had that confidence, but she's happy now. She's also a little rounder, with our baby on the way. It's a killer combination. I love it, and every time I'd bury my face in a new curve, she'd shriek and complain loudly. I almost couldn't let her leave.

Smiling at my desk, I look out the window at the bare winter landscape of the courtyard, thinking of her. This morning as I watched her sleep, I couldn't help breathing a little prayer of thanks. I don't pray, but with that angel in my bed, how could I not? She was curled up facing me, her delicate hand under her chin and her dark hair spread behind her on the pillow.

It was like our own world, secure and full of love. She'd stirred, and meeting her beautiful blue eyes, another quiet thank you echoed through my mind, only this time my memories were on our first encounters. How incredibly sexy she was giving in to me, and how breathless I'd been waiting for her to push me away. She never did.

"How long have you been awake?" She'd touched my cheek then smoothed her fingers into my hair.

"Not long." I'd caught her hand and brought her palm to my lips.

She touched my brow, smoothing it back. "You're less tense than when I got here, and now I have to leave again."

"You forget, I'm trained for periods of separation." Even as I said it, I knew nothing would make telling her goodbye easier.

She pushed up into a sitting position and moved me onto my back. "So being a Marine means you don't miss me?" Her elbows were bent, and one cheek rested on her palm.

I couldn't help laughing at her eyes narrowed in disbelief. I wasn't fooling anyone. "I miss you like the worst pain in the world. Like the desert misses rain."

"That's a song." She kissed me lightly. "And something you have experience with."

Catching her neck, I pulled her forward for a better kiss, but she arched away before I could take it further. "I want to know more about your training. What are your special skills? Besides not missing me when we're apart, of course. Can you fly a plane?"

I shook my head with a chuckle. "Sorry, darling. No piloting for me, but I think Patrick did some flying—"

"I don't believe it. You know things. Tell me!"

Pressing my lips together, my eyes moved down to her chin then to her slim neck where my heart dangled on a thin, gold chain. *Yes, I know things.*

"You keep so many secrets from me," she sighed. "What are you thinking now?"

"The things I know aren't things you want to hear about." Reaching over, I slid my palm over the curve of her waist.

She caught my cheeks in her hands and drew my gaze back. "I want to know everything about you."

For a moment I hesitated. Then my eyes were drawn to the scar, that tiny silver line that starts at the top of her forehead, just above her temple, and disappears into her hairline. "I can kill a man with my bare hands."

Our eyes met again, and I could tell she knew where my thoughts had gone.

"Have you ever done it?"

When I answered her, my voice was quiet. "I've had to kill people."

She hugged herself close against my chest. "I'm sorry. I'm not trying to bring up painful memories. We don't have to talk about it."

Wrapping my arms around her, I pulled her up slightly so I could kiss her neck. "Have I told you how amazing you are?"

A laugh bubbled in her throat. "You always say that. I'm not so amazing."

Rolling us so she was on her back, I looked down into her beautiful face. "You're smart and beautiful. You're incredibly busy, but you make time to show up here—"

"When I know you need me." Leaning down, I kissed her jaw as she continued. "You'd do the same for me. Besides, I can work from anywhere."

"Then work from here."

"You can work anywhere, too."

Our old argument. Neither of us chased it any further—not on our last morning together. We were counting down the hours before we'd be apart again, and instead, I focused on trailing my lips down to her collarbone, past the floating heart, lower to her breasts until we were lost in our special place once more.

Now, sitting at my desk remembering, the only thing strong enough to spoil the afterglow of our weekend is this new case... and her old scar. That damn silver line, a constant reminder of what that fucker did to her. Even worse, it reminds me he's still out there walking around free.

In my line of work, I know how those assholes are. They all have some fucked up notion their victims belong to them—only them. My fist is clenched on the desktop, and I focus on relaxing it.

Sloan will pay for what he did to Mel. I intend to make sure of it, but she's right. Letting him spoil our present gives him too much power. I'd rather put that aside, in my "To Do" file, and focus on my weekend with my little family—sheer red lingerie, loads of sex, and nonstop affection—hell, I should have a shitty week more often.

Shitty week…

I turn to my computer and stare at the report on the screen. As much as Mel wants to know, I can't bring myself to tell her what I'm investigating. It's not that I want to hide my work from her. She could probably help solve half the cases on my desk. I don't want her to be afraid, and I don't have a reason to make her worry yet.

Patrick's in Wilmington watching over her for me, being the guard he is when I'm not there, and I've got tabs on Sloan. We'll know if he leaves the city or makes any threatening moves. Privately, I wish he would. Nothing would make me happier than taking him out in an act of self-defense. With his record, not a jury in the world would convict.

Nikki snaps me out of my reflections. "I'm headed to the coffee shop. Can I get you anything?" She's standing at the door in one of her usual, too-tight wrap-dresses.

It takes me back to her first day here, assigned by my aunt Sue's temp agency. I was still grieving Allison. Three years had passed since my first wife died, but time didn't matter. I didn't want a replacement wife or a girlfriend or an outlet or *anything*, and the idea that my aunt might've selected this woman for any of those reasons got under my skin like nothing else. I didn't need help getting over my wife. I had no intention of getting over her ever, and Nikki's appearance pissed me off.

The reality is, despite her former, inappropriate assertions that I needed to "get laid," she never once made a pass at me. She'd actually seemed more interested in Stuart, my first partner and Patrick's older brother. I suppose after all this time I should put the past behind us. It doesn't make sense anymore now that I have Melissa. Everything has changed.

27

She's waiting, and I exhale. "No. Thank you." The departure from my usual, impatient tone makes her pause, and I continue. "You're always thoughtful, Nikki. I appreciate it."

Her mouth drops open and then quickly closes. "I'm… um… well." She stops stammering, pokes her lips out duck-face style, then nods. "Okay, then. You're welcome."

Turning on a stiletto heel, she heads out of the office, and I grin. That may be the first time I've had Nikki at a loss for words.

Back to my computer, I pull up the file I've been studying for ten days—the one that's had me so distracted. I keep telling Patrick we don't do domestic work, yet I always end up being the one old friends or acquaintances call when they need help.

That's how it started—a runaway case for a friend of a friend.

I was culling through mug shots of beat-up teens and file photos of dead girls. Patrick would say this is the worst part of our job, but truthfully, I don't mind it. I can see past the tragedy to my role here, giving people closure. I know what it's like to need it, and I don't mind helping people get it.

Then I saw *Jessica Black*. Dead.

The name was so familiar, but I couldn't place her at first. Staring at the photo, trying to think, I'd been struck by her appearance—fair complexion, petite frame, and long brunette waves. She looked a lot like Melissa— minus my fiancée's bright blue eyes.

I'd clicked on the thumbnail to read the report. Runaway. Missing five years. Arrested for prostitution several times. Found beaten once. Badly. Now deceased under mysterious circumstances.

Minutes passed as I stared at her photo. Why was she so familiar? She wasn't from Princeton. Her hometown was listed as Raleigh. Shaking my head and chalking it up to overprotectiveness spurred by her similarity to Mel, I closed the document and went back to searching for the runaway.

Nikki had interrupted me that day as well, stopping in with a BLT from the cafeteria.

"I know it's your favorite." She placed the thick sandwich in front of me with a smile. "You need to eat."

I only nodded. "Thanks."

She didn't leave. "Remember the last time I brought you lunch? It was the day Melissa showed up here so angry and unexpected. I was sure I'd never like her, but now she's the sweetest..."

Nikki continued talking, but I wasn't listening. Cold realization flashed in my brain like lightening striking a tree.

Jessica Black. It was the name on the email Melissa had put in front of me that day she visited our offices. The day she dropped a nuke on all my dreams of a life with her, when she revealed my former "mentor," her ex-husband Sloan Reynolds's secret double-life. He had high-end escorts all over the country, and Jessica Black was his first careless slip. Melissa had found it.

Nikki was still reminiscing as I spun around in my chair, shaking my computer awake. Fingers flying over the keys, I pulled up all the information I could find on the dead girl.

She'd been living in Baltimore for a year. I wondered if she followed him from wherever they'd hooked up the first time. *Why would she do that? Was it possible she was in love with him? Was it for the money? Had he promised her anything?*

It didn't matter. She'd disappeared off the police blotter from the time she arrived there until now, when she'd turned up dead.

Reasons scrolled across my brain of all the possible causes of death, but looking at her beaten face, all I could see was the photo Melissa had put in front of me all those months ago.

My instincts were on high alert. Sloan was getting antsy, and I knew what he wanted. Jessica Black might look like the real thing, but she wasn't it.

Substitutes would never fill the possession he felt. I'd followed enough of these twisted fucks to know. He was coming for Melissa, and it was just a matter of when.

All last week, I'd tracked down every misstep I could find on him, looking for anything that would stick, that would get him off the streets or at least keep him in Baltimore. I hoped to find a recent paper trail linking him to Jessica, but every lead came up cold. He was either too slick, or his people buried everything.

Even the guy I had watching Sloan in Baltimore had nothing. Jessica disappeared a week before I'd hired him, a month after Sloan had broken into Mel's beach cottage and then gotten off with a slap on the wrist. Apparently I'd moved too quickly when he waltzed into her home threatening to rape her. We had to wait until he actually committed the crime for his money and position not to matter.

The thought clenched my jaw. It was the one thing above all that caused the "stress" Nikki kept texting Melissa about. Only "stress" wasn't what I felt. What I felt was flat-out fucking rage.

The best part was when he threatened me in court with police brutality charges. I'd nearly brutalized him on the spot, but Melissa held me back. I'll never forget her face. She went still as a stone, as if it was the ending she always expected. It was like a heel-kick straight to my gut. I couldn't let her down that way.

Now all she'll say is she wants those memories left in the past. *Just let it go*, she tells me.

Fuck that. That asshole is a threat to my family, and it's clear he's dangerous. Priority 1 is devising a plan to bring him in, and it has to be something that won't ooze off his slimy back.

Snatching my phone off its base, I hit the speed-dial button.

Patrick answers, cocky as always. "Don't tell me. You've come to your senses and realized life at the beach is the only way to live."

"I need you to up the watch on Melissa."

I appreciate how his tone becomes immediately serious. "What's going on?"

"I have to finish a few details for our new Houston client, and then I'm headed your way, possibly for a while."

"This can only mean one thing. Or one asshole."

"I'm emailing a report and mug shots to you now. The name's Jessica Black." Fingers clicking on the keys, I shoot everything I've found to him. "I've exhausted all my sources here. See if you can do anything from there with it."

"Sure." He's silent for a moment, reading. "Jessica Black... Raleigh? That's just down the road. I'll rattle a few cages."

"If you do find anything, I need to know why she moved to Baltimore. What she was doing there. If she was seeing anybody and who."

"Did you tell Melissa about this?"

Pressing my lips together, I rock back in my chair. "No."

31

"Think that's a good idea?"

"Not really, but I'll tell her when the time is right. I don't want her to be afraid."

Sitting forward again, I pull up the report for our Houston client and read over what's still outstanding. A full system analysis is due Friday. I lost a significant portion of last week searching all the police databases for information on Miss Black.

"If I pull some extra hours, I can have Houston wrapped up and out of here by Wednesday." I start a log on my desktop of what's still outstanding, what jobs are lined up next, and what I can handle from Wilmington in case I can't get back right away.

Nikki's thank you gift can be a week off with pay, maybe a Spa Finder mini-holiday. In the middle of planning my getaway, I realize Patrick is still on the line.

"Sorry to keep you in a holding pattern."

"No worries. I can tell this is serious. Somehow. Even though you haven't told me any details."

Patrick can turn any situation into a joke, and I alternate between being pissed and being glad about it. At the moment, I'm too focused on closing the office and getting to Wilmington to lose time on it.

"I'll tell you everything when I get there. Just keep your eyes on Mel."

"She'll be as protected as the crown jewels."

It doesn't satisfy the tightness in my chest. "Maybe Elaine could invite her to stay in your guest room til Thursday."

"You're joking, right? You know Mel won't leave that cottage without a mandatory evacuation order."

Studying my notes, I wonder how many boxes I'd have to pack if I left for Wilmington today. No, I have to wrap up this damn Houston case here, where I can focus.

Frustrated, I push the laptop back on my desk. "We're professionals, dammit. Get creative."

He laughs. "What would work if you were Melissa? I'd say we invite her over for dinner and mix her drinks too strong, but she's pregnant. And even if she were still drinking, we couldn't keep the party going for three nights. Just tell her what's up."

"If I can be there on Wednesday, I will."

"Fine, but will you at least tell me what's going on? Who is Jessica Black? Or who was, I guess..."

"Jessica Black was a high-end hooker, an escort. She was also one of Sloan's regulars. A few years ago, she was beaten pretty badly, but she wouldn't report the guy. Then she moved to Baltimore. I don't have anything concrete, but my gut says she fell in love with him. How, I can't imagine. Now she's dead."

Silence meets my ear for several moments. When Patrick speaks again, his voice is sober, all joking gone. "And she looks a helluva lot like Melissa."

"Right."

"I know what to do."

In that one sentence I hear my partner lock into closer mode, and it's right where I want him. Patrick can be a royal fuck up when it comes to women, but he's damn good at his job. And to her credit, Elaine seems to have put an end to his screwing around.

"I've got an idea," he continues. "It's something I floated past you a while back, but now with this... Raleigh... I might have a connection to what you need."

"I didn't expect anything less. See you in a few days, and Patrick? Thanks. I owe you one."

"It's nothing more than you'd do for me."

"You know it."

Chapter 3: Backup Plan
Melissa

Eight hours separate Princeton, New Jersey, from Wilmington, North Carolina. Eight long, boring, tedious hours.

I've been hesitant to push the relocation issue on Derek—I want him to be as happy in his hometown as I am in mine—but one more of these long drives, and I might have to rethink that approach.

The only interesting part is keeping track of the cars I pass. One silver Honda seems to always be with me, a few cars behind, but Hondas are pretty common. As tired as I feel, I'm practically seeing double at this point.

Stopping for a fourth bathroom break and to walk around, I'm halfway through Virginia when I send Derek a quick text. *Made it to Richmond. Only four stops this time.*

It doesn't take five seconds for him to text back. *Thanks for letting me know. Never stop in Baltimore without me.*

My nose wrinkles at his overprotectiveness. *The whole city isn't off-limits. Aunt Bea is there.*

Will take you to see her soon. Her cupcakes are my favorite.

I can't help a laugh imagining what my old-fashioned client, a sweet little baker, will say when she meets my fiancé. *She'll love you.*

I love you. You're so beautiful in my bed. It's hard to let you go.

Those words erase all the exhaustion — and the mild irritation at being treated like a china doll. Warmth floods my middle. *I didn't get enough sleep this weekend.*

Wasn't that the point?

Hmm... the point had actually been to find out what's got my future husband so tense and distracted, but between his mouth and my hands and that new red lingerie, that plan had been all but forgotten.

Suddenly the thought of three nights without him seems unbearably lonely. *See you Friday?*

Maybe sooner.

Sooner? A line pierces my forehead.

While I love the idea of not having to wait four whole days to see him, I know he's setting up a new client, and their reports and analyses usually take a month to prepare. Patrick's complained about it before.

I'll explain when I get there. Kiss yourself, kiss baby.

That would be some trick. Love you, Xoxo

Love you more. xxx

I toss the thin phone into my bag and top off my tank before climbing in and getting back on the road. I'm on the Interstate again, and a quick glance to my mirror says Silver Accord is, too. Whatever. Next stop will be my cozy cottage on the most beautiful stretch of beach north of Miami.

My phone buzzes just as I'm pushing through the front door, holding my overnight case and trying to juggle my keys and bag. Inside, I drop everything and look at the face. Elaine. Voicemail dings.

Hitting the button, I put the audio on speaker and set my phone on the counter before unzipping my luggage and digging out my laundry.

"Where are you?" Elaine's bossy, middle-school-teacher voice is a mixture of concern and amusement. "I know, I know. You couldn't leave him. If Derek Alexander convinces you to move eight hours away from me, I'll never speak to either of you again. You know I hated that drive to Baltimore."

And Princeton's even further, I mentally add.

"So I have this whole supper made up for you, and you're going to come over and give me the scoop. I don't want to hear about how tired you are — you were supposed to be home last night. I spent the whole day cooking."

Laughing I shake my head. More like the crock-pot spent the whole day cooking while she was at school.

"Call me. Love you."

Hitting her name on my phone, it doesn't ring once before she answers. "Are you home?"

"Yes, and it was a long drive, and I'm —"

"On your way here to have a nice, comfort-food dinner. I made beef stew, and you don't even have to change. Patrick won't mind."

"Lainey…"

But she's off the phone before I can argue. My stomach grumbles, and I concede. This baby keeps me starving — he'll probably be as big as his daddy — and I don't feel like cooking or eating whatever I can scrape together here.

Catching the strap of my bag, I toss it over the shoulder and head back to the car. At least her place is close.

The savory aroma of celery and garlic, meat and potatoes fills my nose when I open the door. Elaine's got the top off her slow cooker, and the golden boy is right behind her, lifting her light-blonde hair and kissing her neck.

"Okay, knock it off," I complain in a loud, teasing voice.

Elaine drops the lid with a cry and crosses the room to hug me. "How are you feeling?" She leans back and studies my face with a frown. "You look tired."

"I am tired! I told you that." I hug her back. "You dragged me over here, now give me food. And I won't sit and watch you two making out all through dinner."

Patrick leans against the counter smiling at us. His arms are crossed over his lined chest, and he's perfectly handsome in faded jeans and a dark green tee. His sandy-brown hair is shaggy in his hazel eyes.

I've never been happier about my best friend's love life. Elaine used to play it safe when it came to men, which doesn't suit her personality at all. She was miserable with Boring Brian, and I'm glad she took a chance and stepped outside her comfort zone. Patrick is just the sweet bad boy she needs.

"Hey, girl." His voice always sounds like sunshine. "Ginger ale?"

"Sure." I nod, dropping my bag on the counter and allowing Elaine to pull me to the couch in their living room.

"So what did you find out?"

I shake my head as Patrick hands me a white wine glass filled with light amber soda. "Nothing."

"He didn't tell you anything?" Cutting my eyes as I take a sip, she squeals a laugh. "You horny pregnant lady! What exactly were you doing with your mouth all weekend?"

Ginger ale almost comes out my nose. "Shut up!" I pinch her arm and set the glass on the side table.

"Oh, please. You think Patrick's shocked?

He just laughs, going back to the kitchen. "How is the big guy?"

Chewing my bottom lip, I opt for "Energetic."

"No wonder you're so tired. Come on then." My slender friend hops off the couch and pulls me back to the kitchen. "This beef stew I cooked smells delicious."

"Does it count as cooking if you buy all the ingredients premade?"

"Don't be grouchy."

Elaine pulls down three bowls while Patrick slices French bread. He glances up at me. "How was the drive?"

"Long." My elbows are bent, and I rest my forehead on my palms, rubbing away my exhaustion. "I had the strangest feeling…" I shake my head with a little laugh. "I'm sure it was just road fatigue, but I kept thinking I saw the same car behind me the whole way."

Patrick's hand pauses mid-slice, then without a word, he starts cutting again. Elaine's suddenly quiet, and I look around to see what just happened.

"That's silly, right?"

His sunny smile is back in a flash, and Patrick tosses the bread in a bowl. "Yeah. Probably just somebody headed the same direction as you."

—

Right when I turn away, I'm certain I catch a look pass between the two of them, but when I glance back, it's gone. I am seriously exhausted and seeing things.

"You should spend the night here if you're so tired." Elaine puts a steaming bowl of stew in front of me then sets hers at the place across from me where she sits.

Taking the large spoon from beside my bowl, I dip out a carrot from the yummy-smelling broth. "Mmm... I want to sleep in my own bed tonight. But thanks."

Patrick joins us, handing us each a piece of bread before he sits. I rip out the center of mine and dunk it in the dark brown gravy. "This really is delicious. Thanks for making me come over."

Elaine exhales a little laugh and then falls silent, eating. We're all three pretty quiet, which is unusual for our group. I'd complain if I weren't feeling sleep trying to roll over me in giant waves. Instead, I take another warm bite of savory meat.

"At least let me drive you home, then," Elaine says.

I shake my head. "Then my car would be over here, and you've got school—"

"I'll spend the night."

"Then I'd have to get up and drive you back in the morning before school." Shaking my head, I lift my soft-drink-holding wine glass and sip. "I'll be fine, and I want to sleep in tomorrow."

Patrick stands and goes briefly into the kitchen before returning with his phone, which he sets on the table between him and Elaine. My bowl is now empty, and I'm just about to announce my departure when it buzzes. Elaine's head turns, and she snatches it up, springing out of her chair.

"Toni Durango?" Her voice is too loud. "Who the HELL is Toni Durango? Patrick! What the FUCK? Is this a stripper?"

I'm fully awake now, and completely bewildered at both the volume of her voice and what she's saying.

"Lainey—" Patrick stands, but she cuts him off.

"NO!" She shoves the phone hard into his chest. He tries to catch her but she pushes him again. Elaine is unusually strong, take it from me. "I'm not listening to your bullshit! Fuck you, Patrick!"

She storms to the bedroom, and I'm frozen in my spot. My mouth is open, and I'm sure I look like a guppy. *Would a stripper call Patrick? How would she have his number? Did Patrick give his number to a stripper? Could it be part of a case?*

He doesn't wait for me to intervene. He's headed to the bedroom after her, just as a heavy, black combat boot flies through the opening. I scream and he ducks, avoiding the headshot.

"Honey... Don't throw things at my head." Somehow his voice sounds scolding instead of pleading.

"Don't touch me!" Elaine's still yelling, and my heart's beating too fast. I've never liked confrontations like this, but I hesitate before leaving.

"Lainey?" My voice is high and soft, and I stand, cautiously going toward the bedroom. I don't want to be hit by any flying objects either, and my coordination isn't as good as it was pre-pregnancy. "Are you okay?"

A flash of blonde hair, and she's out of the bedroom, cheeks pink and a small suitcase in her hand. "I'm staying with you tonight. Let's go."

"Uhh..." I'm certain I could win the Most Helpless Award at that moment.

Patrick goes to the fireplace and rubs the back of his neck as he studies the orange flames. I watch as my best friend storms past me and out the door.

"Okay, then." I shake my head and follow her, picking up my bag. Elaine's already in my car, sitting with her arms crossed, when I open the driver's side door.

"Honey?" I have no idea what to say right now. These guys are not having problems. It's impossible.

"Just stop. Patrick was a player before we got together, so what makes me think he'd stop being a player now?"

"Because he loves you? Because he left everything in Princeton behind to be here with you? Is it possible you're being a little hasty?"

I can't tell if she's about to cry or not. Somehow it doesn't seem like she is. With a deep exhale, I get in and push the key into the ignition. I almost jump out of my skin when she shrieks again.

"Wait!"

"You're going to send me into premature labor—"

"Forgot my glasses." She's out the car and running back inside as I sit in the idling vehicle.

My shoulders drop as she disappears through the door. This whole situation is weird. Elaine isn't flighty, nor does she jump to conclusions. And from what I've observed, she has Patrick whipped pretty well.

I continue waiting, wondering what the hell's taking so long, when a low throb like heartburn starts in the center of my chest.

What if she is right, and Patrick *is* cheating or whatever? He always seemed so sweet to me. The self-doubt creeping up the back of my neck is even worse than the *déjà vu* of being watched. I think Patrick is a great guy. I also thought Sloan was a great guy. Is my ability to judge character still so warped?

I think Derek's a great guy...

Elaine's back, jumping into my car before I can go any further on that crazy-train of mentally exhausted thought. In the brief, dome light, her lips appear pink and slightly swollen… like she's been kissing someone. Then it's dark again.

"Let's go," she snaps.

That does it. "Don't be all bossy with me. I don't know any strippers." Now I'm frowning.

"I'm sorry." She drops back against the passenger seat and turns to face me. "Thanks for letting me sleep over. It can be like a girls' night."

I shake my head. "I'm going to bed when we get home. You can work out whatever this is on your own."

I'm asleep before my head meets the pillow. Elaine's snug in my little guest room, and as yet, she still hasn't shed a tear. She doesn't even seem mad anymore.

I'm about to accuse them both of pulling some inexplicable role-playing stunt, but I hesitate. I could be wrong.

Still, I know my friend has a wild side. I'm just too tired to delve into it tonight. Lainey's like my sister, and if she needs to crash here, that's fine. We'll sort it out tomorrow.

Somewhere past midnight, I wake with a jolt. The house is quiet, but I throw back the covers and go to my bedroom door. My heart is beating so fast as I pause and listen, but everything sounds peaceful. *What was it?*

I stand a few moments in groggy silence, trying to remember what might've woken me. It's been a while since I've slept on edge, sleep so near waking it could hardly qualify as restful, and it often involved clutching that small can of pepper spray under my pillow. It was how I usually slept when I lived in Sloan's house.

Elaine's voice comes from the guest room, so I tiptoe down the hall. The yellow-pine floor is soft and warm beneath my feet in spite of the cold, and the cottage is

---

new enough that nothing creaks. I'm quiet as a cat sneaking around.

"I swear I heard something." Her voice is a shaky whisper. She pauses, listening to whoever's on the line... I'm pretty certain I know who it is. "Maybe." Pause. "I guess I was asleep, but come over and spend the night anyway." More waiting as she listens. "We'll worry about that tomorrow. I need you here."

Rolling my eyes at the pleading tone in her voice, I'm fully prepared to find Patrick in my kitchen in the morning. They're both about to make my shit list for whatever's going on. Still, I'm smiling as I crawl back into my bed.

Lainey's not used to being here, and I'm not used to overnight guests in that little room. We most likely disturbed each other, but I'll sleep better with Patrick here. And the truth is, I'm relieved to know they're okay, no matter what I witnessed at their condo tonight. I drift back to sleep, my shaky self-confidence restored.

Sure enough, Derek's business partner is standing in my kitchen when I stagger in for coffee the next morning. He's in a white tee and the same faded jeans, and he's cute as ever with his messy bedhead and scruffy cheeks.

"Good morning," I say with a squint. "I guess we're all made up again?"

"Hey, babe." He steps forward and pecks my forehead. "Sleep okay?"

"All except for a few moments after midnight..."

His body goes on visible defense. "Did you hear something?"

I feel like I'm calming a German Shepherd. "I heard Elaine on the phone begging you to come over."

His broad shoulders drop. "Oh."

44

Jamming my hands on my hips, my voice is raised now. "What the hell is going on here? First Derek's wound so tight, now you and Elaine are acting like... I don't know what. Like you're auditioning for community theater—"

"Hang on." He steps toward me and then looks around.

"She's still in the guest room, but she'll be flying in here any minute. She has to be at school in an hour."

He catches me by the shoulders and pulls me further into the kitchen. "Just between us, okay?"

I nod, unsure what he's about to say.

"Derek wants to tell you himself. So just be cool."

He's quiet again, and it actually appears he's done. That's it. All I get.

I push his hands off me. "What! That's the most... I thought you were about to tell me something I can use."

"And risk the wrath of Derek? No fucking way. That's one ass-kicking I've somehow managed to avoid, and I plan to keep it that way." He laughs, and turns to the fridge, pulling out the OJ. "But Elaine's spending the night with you until he gets here, okay?"

"Which means you are, too?"

He grins and does a little shrug.

I'm frustrated, and my throat feels tight. "This doesn't make any sense unless he's afraid of me being alone... which means—"

In that instant it all clicks together. It couldn't be anything else, and I feel like an idiot for not seeing it sooner. At the same time, my stomach drops as I acknowledge what it means.

Just then Elaine flies into the kitchen, as predicted, whizzing around the room and gathering her things fast. She sees me and freezes, guilt filling her green eyes. "You're awake."

45

"And you two aren't really fighting."

Her pink lips twist, but a car horn sounds outside. "Oh, that's my ride. Sorry, Mel. Have to get to school." She pecks me on the cheek and Patrick on the mouth — followed by him grabbing her waist and pulling her back for a longer, open-mouthed smooch.

I leave the kitchen, headed for my bedroom with a boulder in my chest. The case that has Derek so tense, Patrick turning into my live-in babysitter... I'm standing by my bedside thinking when it all clicks together.

"You okay?"

I squeal and almost throw my coffee across the bed. "Patrick! Jesus!"

He tries not to laugh, putting a hand on my shoulder. "That's exactly what he wants to avoid. He doesn't want you to be afraid."

My heart's still flying as I set my coffee cup on the dresser. "So you're really not going to tell me what's happening?"

"No."

Dropping onto the bed, I look up at him. "How long will you two be staying here?"

"Until Derek arrives on Thursday."

Thursday. Despite it all, knowing he'll be here so soon makes my heart rise. "That performance last night really wasn't necessary. You could've just insisted I spend the night."

"It was a last-ditch effort." He walks over and sits beside me on the bed, patting my knee. "We tried everything to get you to stay at our place. You're stubborn as a damn mule."

"I am not!" My eyes widen, and he laughs more.

"Have you met yourself?"

I want to laugh, but my realization kills the levity. "This is about Sloan, isn't it?"

46

Patrick's smile fades, and he looks down. No answer.

The truth of what's going on beats painfully in my chest. The change must be clear on my face because in one quick move, his arms are around my shoulders, and I'm pulled into Patrick's embrace.

"It's going to be okay." His voice is soothing, his hug warm. "I've got you covered until Derek gets here, and then he'll take over."

"I'm fine." I push back and clear my throat. "Sloan doesn't scare me anymore. Look." Going to the closet, I open the door and reach inside, pulling out a wooden baseball bat. "Backup plan."

His grin returns at the sight of it. "Think you could use it on him?"

"I know I could use it on him."

He walks over to me. Then he taps me on the nose with the tip of his finger. "Glad to hear it, because I have to drive to Raleigh today. I'm pretty certain you'll be okay while I'm gone, but I feel a little better now."

A line pierces my forehead. "What's in Raleigh?"

"Not what, who. Toni Durango."

"The stripper?" I'm right behind him as he heads to the door. "Elaine was right?"

He pauses before leaving. "No and yes. No, she's not a stripper. She's a former escort. And yes, Elaine knows. I'm hoping she'll help us. Wish me luck."

"Don't get lucky!"

"Too late."

My mouth drops open as I watch him climb in the waiting Charger and drive away. The sound of my phone buzzing snaps me out of it, and I see a text from Derek.

Sleep well?

I pick up the device and quickly type back. *Two house guests last night. You've got some explaining to do.*

See you soon.

We exchange *I love you; I love you mores,* and it appears that's as much information as I'm going to get. And it's pissing me off.

Chapter 4: A Physical Reminder
Derek

Fucking Houston took longer than I planned.

Between filtering through their myriad of networks and users and their lax social media policy, half the computers had viruses and the other half had unnecessary virus protection added. I don't finish the analysis until late Wednesday.

Nikki is sitting at the front desk waiting, perky as ever, when I present her with the package.

"Happy leap year." Keeping the frustration out of my voice is difficult.

"What's this, boss?"

Remembering my new leaf, I soften my tone. "I need you to mail that to our new Houston client. And I've got a surprise for you."

Her dark brow arches.

"Take the rest of the week off. With pay."

Instead of squealing, she leans back in her chair. "Is it that bad?"

I feel my own brow furrow in response. "What?"

"Look, I know you think I'm just a dumb blonde, but you're wrong. Something's going on, and it's something with Melissa."

For a split second, I almost lose it, but I recover fast — poker face back in place. "Melissa's fine."

"I know she's fine. We text pretty regularly. But whatever has you so edgy is about her, and don't try to tell me it isn't."

Fuck. The tension creeps up my back again.

Why didn't I go solo after Stuart left? Patrick was a real test of my patience, but Nikki might push me over the cliff. I don't need an office manager. I handle my own travel plans now, and half the time I even answer my own damn phone.

But Melissa likes her.

"I'm working on something," I say, calming the adrenaline spike in my veins. "And I'm handling it. There's no need to worry Melissa."

Her blue eyes roam around my face searching for clues. Nikki has pretty much pissed me off since Day 1, but if she can keep her mouth shut now, I'll let all of it go.

We face each other for a few, tense seconds before she nods. "I won't say anything."

"Thank you."

"Only because I know how much you love her. You'll do anything to protect her. Right?"

I can't believe she even has to ask, but I guess some women see a lot more shitty guys than good ones. "Right. I won't be back in this office until I'm sure she's safe."

Standing, she collects her coat, purse, and the package. Then she gives me a little salute. "Take as long as you need, boss. I'll be on standby if you want someone here."

And with that, she's out the door. I lean against her desk, gauging my level of exhaustion. If I leave now, I'll be in Wilmington by morning. If I fall asleep at the wheel, I won't be any use to anybody. My phone buzzes, and when I see the face, I make my decision.

PM check in! Melissa texts. P&E are here. *You home or work?*

Just finished Houston, leaving work. Miss you.
Tomorrow?
ASAP.
Be careful driving. Love you.
Love you more.

The cottage is dark when I arrive at 6 a.m. Elaine is the only one with an early wake-up call, so it's possible I can get into Melissa's room before they're up and stirring. Driving all night might not have been the most restful approach, but with the energy surging through my chest, I knew I wouldn't get any sleep anyway. I'll nap a few hours this morning and be ready to go without losing a day.

Dropping my duffel by the stainless fridge inside, I ease off my boots and place them one at a time by the door doing my best to keep quiet. Grabbing a water bottle, I head to Melissa's bedroom, but I nearly slam it against the skull of a half-dressed Patrick. He's right around the corner, holding a wooden baseball bat high, like he's about to use my head for the winning homer in the World Series.

"*SHIT!*" we both whisper-shout.

"What the fuck?" Patrick lowers the bat and breathes.

I recognize the energy surging through his muscles. It matches the rapid tweaking of my own, and I need a second to recover.

"You could've shot me a text," he groans, dropping onto the couch. "Did you fucking drive all night?"

"Couldn't sleep." I clap his shoulder as I pass. "Glad to see you're on your toes. You're officially off guard duty."

"Hey!" I pause, and he tosses me the bat. "Happy to help. I'm going back to bed."

Catching his "weapon," my brow lines. "Think you'll be able to sleep?"

"Nope." That grin spreads across his face. It's the same one that used to tick me off because I knew it meant I'd be cleaning up his shit sooner rather than later.

"Just keep it down. I don't need to hear you getting any."

He points back at me as he heads down the hall. "Right back atcha."

Shaking my head, I turn Melissa's bedroom door handle as softly as possible. Unlike my younger partner, I don't plan to wake her this early. I know the pregnancy makes her tired, and I'll be content to be beside her. It'll be the first good rest I've had in four days, knowing she's with me and safe.

She's curled in her familiar sleeping position, and I can't help a smile as the warmth of love fills me. I will never get tired of watching this woman sleep.

Jeans off, I whip the thin, navy sweater I'm wearing over my head and slip into her king-sized bed. She doesn't even stir, and I'm happy she feels so secure with Patrick in the house. He might have been a pain in my ass in the past, but he's more than made up for it with this assignment.

Easing closer to her, I lift her long, dark waves off the pillow and replace them with my head. She makes a soft noise and stirs, but she doesn't wake. My arm goes above her, and our bodies are so close, I can feel the warmth radiating from her ivory skin.

Wrapping a dark curl around my finger, the tension slowly drains from my body. Being with her is enough. She's home and comfort and warmth and all the good things I thought I'd never have again. She's my future and my desire and my love, and the notion that some dickwad might try to hurt this woman, might threaten what I cherish...

She sighs and scoots closer to me, still asleep. The idea that she knows I'm here is incredibly satisfying. My own eyes are heavy, and I lower my head.

In three breaths, I'm out.

It's dark, and I sense his presence. He's hiding like the coward he is, waiting for me to let my guard down so he can strike, so he can try to hurt her again.

Sensations of being back in battle engage my reflexes. I can't see the enemy, but that doesn't mean he can't see me. I have to move forward, keeping the one I'm charged to protect covered by my side.

A noise, and I know where he is. My fists are clenched. This time I'm not sure I'll have the presence of mind to stop until he's eliminated. Permanently.

Energy is building in my core, preparing for a fight... And the scene changes.

Softest velvet touches my skin. Whispers like a butterfly's wings feather over my cheeks and the sensation moves to my brow. Now it's on my temple, causing my eyes to blink open.

I'm in Melissa's pale green room. Sloan's gone, and the butterfly wings are her hair falling in my face as her delicate lips cover me with kisses.

One swift movement, and she's on her back with a shriek and a laugh. I want to cover her mouth with mine, but first I'd like to swish with some water — or preferably mouthwash. Instead I opt for devouring her slim neck.

Her fingers thread into the sides of my hair. "What time did you get in?" Her voice is breathy and high, as I follow a trail with my lips along her collarbone.

"Just before six. I tried not to wake you." My mouth is moving up into her hair, behind her ear. She smells like roses mixed with the ocean, and I inhale deeply as she makes one of those little noises I love.

"Patrick said he almost batted you into next week." A laugh moves through her torso.

"He did a fantastic job." I kiss her jaw, pulling little bits of skin between my teeth, tasting her. She's delicious. "I'm giving him a bonus. Something major. A Rolex."

She's squirming, trying to catch my lips with hers, and I lift up long enough to grab the water bottle and take a quick hit, swishing it around and then diving back into her arms. She pushes my shoulders, flipping me onto my back and straddling my waist as she forces my lips apart, finding my tongue.

She's wearing a skirt, and the way she's sitting, I can tell she's not wearing panties. Fuck me. Her heat is flush on my bare stomach, and between that, her hands in my hair, and her mouth moving mine, my morning wood has turned into a full-fledged tree — one of those giant redwoods.

"You're overdressed." I pull up the sweater she's wearing, and my brow collapses with appreciation when I discover she's also braless.

Her breasts are firm and round and a few sizes bigger these days. *Gorgeous*.

Holding them, I massage my thumbs over the dark circles before pulling a beaded nipple into my mouth. She lets out a moan, and the chances are great I'll last about as long as a teenage boy once I'm inside her.

Melissa is not helping the situation. She slides down my stomach and jerks my boxer briefs to my hips. The beast is unleashed, and she covers it with that hot velvet mouth.

"Fuck." I arch back and try to think of baseball. Cold showers. House fires…

Her small hand pumping my shaft. Warm lips caressing my tip then moving lower, followed by the slow sweep of her tongue. *Shit*.

In a move fast enough to rival Superman, I catch her under the arms and pull her up and over. I'm inside, sinking deep into her slippery-wet body, in less than two seconds.

"Derek!" She cries and holds on, but I can't stop.

She's lying on her back, but I'm on my knees leaning into her, needing to be as deep inside her as possible. Her moans drive me crazy as I grip her ass, pulling her against me. *Harder, faster…* My stomach tightens as the explosion builds. A ragged groan scrapes my throat as the orgasm blazes through me, shaking me to the core. It's so good, I have to hold her a few moments to recover.

Releasing my grip on her backside, I lean on the headboard as I catch my breath. These last several weeks, I've been doing my best to avoid putting pressure on her abdomen, where the baby is, but she's crawling up, lips following the lines on my stomach, kissing her way up my chest until she wraps her arms around my neck.

"You're so sexy when you let go." Her voice is a husky whisper, and when I open my eyes, her beautiful mouth is inches from mine. I can't resist kissing it.

"You didn't finish. I'm sorry."

Her blue eyes narrow, making her look even more like the sex kitten she is right now. "I guess you have to make it up to me then."

I manage a weak laugh. "You might have to give me a minute."

She makes a teasing pout that melts into a smile she presses against my lips. Her breasts touch my chest, and it's possible I might have a little something left.

My hands roam down her sides, exploring her curves. She's still up, but I move lower, kissing the sexy crease at the bottom of one breast, inhaling the scent of her body. Fresh-air flowers.

"Mmm..." The vibration of her voice moves through her torso as I kiss her skin. My fingers go between her legs, my thumb circling the tiny bud while my middle fingers push inside her. She moans again, and her hips rock as she rides my hand. I catch her up with a few practiced movements.

Her eyes are closed as she savors the sensations. Her nipples bounce near my chin, so I pull one into my mouth, which earns me another little cry.

"Derek, oh..." Her sighing my name like that is enough to get my semi all the way to ready, and I lie back, pulling her onto my lap so she can ride it out.

Her hips buck against mine as her hair swishes around her waist, and I'm glad I got the edge off because I wouldn't miss this sight for the world. Her gorgeous body is like a goddess rising above me, sexy and full of life. I'm holding back now, enjoying the beauty of her ecstasy. She's mine to cherish and to love and to protect, and if my past has taught me anything, it's how to do that.

Her insides are pulling me, massaging and milking, and now my own instincts kick in. I catch her waist, rocking my hips against her.

"Yes... oh, shit!" She wails, shoulders shuddering with my thrusts, and with a groan, I let go.

It's pure bliss the second time I come. One last push, and she collapses in my arms, a broad smile on her face. Her cheek is on my shoulder and she starts to giggle.

"What?" Smoothing back her hair, I smile as her blue eyes blink open.

"That was incredible." Then she laughs again. "I'm such a stereotype. The horny pregnant lady."

Kissing her eyes and face, I hug her close against me. "You're not a stereotype. You're amazingly sexy and everything I want."

She stretches up and kisses my nose. "I thought I'd have to wait a while after that first round."

"No way." My hand is cupping her breast, my thumb circling her nipple. "I can't have my lady frustrated."

"Thank you." Then she giggles again, sitting back and wrapping the sheet around her body, eyes sparkling. "Saying that makes me think of our first time. I was sure I'd gone crazy being with a complete stranger like that. And then you thanked me."

She covers her eyes and laughs again. I love seeing her so happy.

"You have no idea what a game-changing moment that was for me. It was pretty major." My thoughts go back to the reason for that encounter and the reason I'm here with her now, and my tone grows serious. "You were always safe with me. I'm sure you sensed it even then."

Another laugh and she shakes her head, dropping her chin. "I'm pretty sure the only thing I sensed was how incredibly sexy you are."

Catching that chin, I rub my thumb over her soft skin. "I should've done better research before agreeing to help him."

"Stop." Her hand covers mine, pulling it down and threading our fingers. "We've covered that. And anyway, if you had done better research, you probably would've turned him down, and we'd have never met. It was ultimately for the best."

I can't argue with that.

"Now," she continues. "Since we've caught up physically—"

"I wouldn't be so sure—"

She dodges my attempt to pull her to me again. "Tell me why I've had house guests all week. Why you're here early. It's about my ex-husband, isn't it?"

Her attempt at being bossy is adorable. "What makes you think that?"

"Patrick is a terrible liar."

"There goes his Rolex."

I start to get up, but she catches my arm and holds me. "Tell me what's going on."

Her blue eyes are serious, and I sit back against the headboard again. "Okay, yes. It's about Sloan, and this time I'm not giving up until he's behind bars."

Or in hell, I mentally add.

Anger or frustration—it's hard to tell which— flashes across her face. "I told you I wanted to put the past behind us."

"I'd be happy to do that if he weren't still a threat."

"What threat?" Her voice goes high. "He's back in Baltimore. He wouldn't dare touch me. Sloan's pretty sick, but he's not stupid enough to cross you."

"I wish I could agree, but I've seen too many cases like this. I know how they go."

She tries to leave the bed, but I catch her and bring her back. "You have to trust me on this, Mel."

"You mean I have to live in fear all the time, looking over my shoulder? I won't do it. I can't."

"I'm not asking you to live in fear."

"And I won't have you jeopardizing our future by doing something potentially illegal just to... what? Get revenge?"

My lips tighten at her words. I know she's saying these things because she wants to convince me, but she's only partially informed. Reaching up, I rest my palm on the side of her face and run my thumb lightly over her scar.

"Every time I see this, I want to kill him. I know exactly how I'll do it, too."

She reaches up to take my hand and fold it in both of hers. "My scar reminds me of how strong I am. What I can survive."

A familiar anger tightens in my chest that she would even need a physical reminder of such a thing.

"I wish I'd never shown you that picture." Her voice is quiet as she traces her fingertip over the back of my hand. "It was unfair, and now you can never un-see it."

"Jessica Black is dead."

Her body goes still. For a moment I'm not sure if she's breathing.

"Mel?"

Now when her eyes travel up to mine, they're worried. "How..."

"I don't know, but I have a hunch."

Blinking quickly, her head moves side to side as she's processing what I'm not saying. "He didn't... he wouldn't..." She squeezes her blue eyes closed, and I'm worried she'll cry. She doesn't. Instead when she opens her eyes this time acceptance is in her voice. "But why?"

"Have you ever seen a picture of her?"

"I never saw pictures of any of them."

"I'd be willing to bet they all have a similar look, and it's long, dark waves, petite with fair skin."

She's off the bed now, scooping up my shirt and wrapping it around her body. Her arms are crossed over her midsection, and she's pacing the room still shaking her head. "No. He's an abusive, controlling son of a bitch, but he's not a murderer."

Picking up my jeans, I quickly step in and pull them up my hips before crossing the room to pull her into my arms. "You say that, but you didn't believe he'd hurt you either."

I feel the tremors moving through her, and I hug her tighter against my chest. "Shh... I'm here now, and I'm not leaving until he's no longer a threat to you. Or the baby."

Another shiver moves through her, but she's fighting it. "Do you have some reason to believe he's responsible? The girl was a hooker. She lived a dangerous life. She could've been killed for any number of reasons."

"She was living in Baltimore. She'd moved there a year ago, and it appears she was one of Sloan's regulars. It's probably why he got careless, and you found out."

"That's a big leap with no evidence."

"Police records have a mug shot of her beaten. It's what caught my attention in the first place. The image looks... very similar to what you showed me."

"Oh, god." She covers her face with her hands.

Guiding her back to the bed, we sit on the foot. I pull her onto my lap and wrap my arms around her, preparing to hold her for as long as she needs. Not surprisingly, it isn't very long.

She pushes back and seems to shake herself. Standing again, I see her find that strength I know is inside her. It's amazing to watch.

"Fuck him." Her voice is calm. "Let Sloan Reynolds try to come here. I have a Louisville slugger for that very purpose."

Grinning, now I'm the one shaking his head. "I love you so much, and there is no fucking way I'll let you be a sitting duck out here."

She stops moving and faces me, hands on hips. "So you have a plan? Patrick's in on it?"

"Yeah. I'm heading to Raleigh with him to meet someone he says will help us."

"Toni Durango. You're hiring a hooker."

"He really lost that Rolex this time."

"I saw the name on his phone. He told me what she does."

Standing, I cross to where she is and put my hands on the tops of both her shoulders. "I don't know what Sloan might do, but at this point, I'm willing to consider any possibility. After last week, I was willing to hire someone to take care of him for me—"

"Don't let him win." Her eyes are round and serious. "If he took you away from me, I'd have lost something I can't live without."

"Enter Patrick, our man with the plan."

"And his friendly call girl."

A little groan rises in my throat. "I'll let you know how it goes. I haven't committed to anything yet."

Chapter 5: American Muscle
Derek

The Skinniflute saloon is about the type of dive I'd expect from a Patrick source. A wood-paneled biker joint with perforated steel plates on the lower half each exterior, the only windows are small and near the ceiling, and the dark interior is lit by single-bulbs hanging over the small booths lining the walls. Fluorescent lights and neon beer signs add illumination behind the bar in the center of the room.

As instructed, I'm wearing dark jeans, boots, and an inconspicuous black tee and leather jacket. Patrick's in a similar getup, but he's added a bandanna tied over his light brown hair.

"Should I be expecting a fight?" I quip as we slide into the wooden booth to wait for Toni.

"Hell, no. These guys are pretty mellow. Didn't even look up last time I was in here."

"How often are you in here?"

He shrugs. "Third time."

A waitress, who resembles Amy Winehouse in hot pants and a tight sweater, appears with a small, round tray. Her dark eyes move quickly from Patrick to do a slow sweep over me. I don't return her interest.

"Hey, Brian. What can I getcha?"

My eyes cut across the table to my partner's. "Vodka rocks and this guy will have..."

"Coke is fine. I'm driving."

Her eyebrows rise, and she spins on her heel before sashaying away. I'm pretty sure her exaggerated hip movements are for our benefit.

When she's far enough away, I lean forward on the table. "Brian?"

"First time I was here, I didn't want Toni to know I was looking for her, so I told Lylah my name was Brian."

"Lylah?"

"Just go with it."

We straighten up as she returns to put the drinks in front of us. Patrick puts a twenty on her tray. "Keep an eye on this for me."

"You got it, babe."

She saunters off again, and I settle in to wait for our contact. "So you've explained the situation to Toni?"

Patrick shrugs. "Only in a roundabout way. I wasn't sure how much you wanted out there, but she's willing to help us. She has some bad blood she wasn't ready to tell me about on Tuesday."

"Maybe she'll talk about it now."

I glance up as another brunette enters the bar. She's tall and slim and dressed similarly to Lylah. I wonder if it's the standard uniform for this place.

"Yeah, that's her." Patrick follows my gaze, and I see their eyes connect.

A slight nod, and she says something to Lylah before heading in our direction.

My lips curl into a frown. "She's too tall."

"She likes to wear those stilts." Sure enough, she's wearing stripper heels.

"Do you have a shoe fetish or something?"

Patrick gives me The Smile. "Nothing's hotter than a naked woman in heels."

Lifting the Coke, I can't resist a small jab. "Especially when she's got your dick in her mouth."

"Nope." He shakes his head, serious again. "Elaine's the only woman for me now."

"You've got some incredible good luck, partner."

"Don't I know it." He slides down as Toni approaches the table.

Her eyes graze over me as she takes the spot Patrick's created, and she returns my frown. "You look like a judgmental asshole." Her voice is low and smoky.

This is getting worse by the second, and I'm losing interest fast. "And you look like every con artist I've ever helped put away."

"Well," Patrick laughs, doing his best to salvage things. "This is getting off to a great start. Can I get you a drink?"

She shakes her head. "I'm on the clock. What's this about, Patrick?"

"My partner here…" He pauses for introductions. "Derek Alexander, Toni Durango…"

We nod, still displeased at the prospect of working together. Patrick continues. "My partner here has a problem, and I think you can help. It's about the situation we discussed on Tuesday."

Pushing a lock of straight, dyed-black hair off her shoulder, she takes a sip of his vodka. "You didn't tell me much, and I only said I'd listen. I haven't agreed to work with anybody."

He nods. "Fair enough. Derek? You want to explain the situation?"

It makes sense, as I know more about what's going on than anybody. "It's like this…" But my phone cuts me off. It emits the special tone I've set up for my man in Baltimore, and I pull it out fast to read the screen, my current meeting forgotten.

Subject AWOL. Sorry, boss, he must've left in the night. Can't find him.

I'm on my feet before I've even finished reading, swiping Patrick's keys off the table.

"Derek?" Somewhere behind me, I feel Patrick struggling to get Toni out of the booth so he can follow, but I'm in a tunnel. My brain is miles away, focused on one objective — getting back to Wilmington. Fast.

I'm out the door with my heart thundering painfully. Jamming the key into the ignition, Patrick's Charger roars to life. Satisfaction surges through my legs. It's going to be a tough drive, but for once I'm thankful for Patrick's bravado. American muscle is exactly what I need to cover the miles at top speed.

Shoving the stick into reverse to back out, I slam on the breaks and put it in gear before punching it. Rocks fly as I spin out of the lot, and I only vaguely hear Patrick yelling for me to wait. He'll figure out a ride back. I've got to get to Melissa.

I try calling her, but it goes to voicemail. I send her a quick text. *Call me please.*

While I wait, I hit Elaine's number, voicemail. She's in class. I try Mel's mother, voicemail again. *Dammit!* She's probably with a patient. Why don't I have her office number programmed in my phone?

I throw my cell on the passenger seat and grip the wheel again. Both hands hold it so hard, I'm surprised it doesn't bend in half. It's like my body is trying to push the car faster by brute force.

How could I be so careless? Bennett's been watching Sloan for weeks, and nothing's happened. He's been quiet, going about his routine, obeying the law. I should've known he'd make a move now.

Melissa said his behavior was cyclical, and she could tell when it was time for him to either leave town for a hook-up or for her to start sleeping with her door locked and the can of pepper spray under her pillow. The very thought of her living like that grinds my jaw.

After all my work closing the office, driving all night, I left her alone, out there in that little cottage unguarded. *Fuck*! My fists tighten harder on the thin, metal ring guiding Patrick's sports car. I'm pushing ninety, and car after car flashes past.

Traffic is light this early-afternoon Thursday. It's the one small advantage I have. I'm making the most of it and wishing I had a portable siren. Once more the smallest prayer sneaks from my brain. *Not again. Please don't let it happen again.*

I'm too far from her. If she needs me, if she's afraid or in danger, I'm not there. If the unthinkable happens… Memories of the pain of that loss scorch through my chest. The mind-numbing helplessness is back. I can't bear it a second time. I can't lose Melissa.

Glancing down, I'm at a hundred now. I'll be there soon, but it still feels too long. My breath is fast, and my brain is repeating the word No. It's all I've got, the force of my will, demanding that she be okay.

CHAPTER 6: FIRST PRIORITY
MELISSA

Working from home at the beach is possibly the absolute best outcome I could've ever imagined. Waking up to find Derek in my bed only makes it a million times better.

Leaning back on my sun porch as the waves crash a short distance away, I smile warmly remembering our incredible morning. Now he needs to stop being so stubborn and relocate.

It's chilly, and I'm wearing fleece pants, a long-sleeved red tee with a fuzzy blanket wrapped around my shoulders. In my thick socks, I'm cozy enough to nap, but I'm working on a marketing plan for Aunt Bea to take her cupcake bakery online. She's completely baffled by how it all works, of course, but with her skills and built-in clientele, she'll take off in no time.

I've just hit *send* on the email explaining it to her in as simple terms as possible, then I wrap the cozy blanket a bit tighter around my shoulders and drift into a pleasant slumber, hoping that when I wake, my sweet love will be by my side again.

My sleep is troubled, and even with the blanket, I shiver. A sound like scissors flicks near my ear, and I flinch. *Cutting... Something's cutting... My hair?*

No, that's wrong.

The expression "someone walked over my grave" drifts through my hazy brain, and I feel so afraid, I might cry.

Derek... where is Derek? I need him here. I need him to protect me.

It doesn't matter if I tell him I'm strong, and I can take care of myself. I'm afraid. The terror holding me won't let go, and all I want is my big man.

It's dark. My heart is thundering in my chest, and with a cold certainty, I recognize the sound of his footsteps, the spicy smell of his cologne. It stings my nose and makes my throat close up.

Sloan.

He's here.

I can't catch my breath.

The baby. I have to protect the baby...

Footsteps pound louder, closer, and with a loud gasp, I bolt upright on the couch.

But I'm alone.

It was just a dream.

"Oh, my god!" My trembling hand goes over my face, and I can't stop the tears streaming down my cheeks.

"Melissa?" Apparently the footsteps weren't a dream. Derek bursts through the side door, and without hesitation, I fly off the couch into his arms. Instantly they surround me as he kisses my head, speaking against my hair. "You're okay. I'm here now. You're safe."

His voice is tense as he holds me tightly, and gradually, my shaking calms. He eases me back and bends down to look in my eyes. "What happened? Why are you crying?"

Even though his voice is soothing, his entire body is on edge. His muscles seem larger, like he's ready to fight. That's when I find my strength. Shaking myself, I place my palms flat against my cheeks.

"I'm sorry." *Breathe, Melissa, breathe.* "I... I had the most vivid dream. I thought someone was here... I-It scared me."

My fingers curl, and he holds me close again. I bury my face in his chest, and the last of my terror slowly recedes.

Derek isn't satisfied. He covers me with the blanket. "I'm going to look around, make sure you weren't picking up on something in your sleep."

He steps to the screen door and turns the little latch, locking it. My brow lines. "What do you mean? Did you see something?"

His face is stoic, but it softens with a smile when he glances down at me. "No, but I want to check the place out just in case," touching my cheek lightly, "you're very attuned to your surroundings."

"For a while I had to be."

He continues into the house, his mouth in a firm line. I stay on the couch, pulling the soft blanket tightly as I wait.

It's later in the afternoon than I normally nap, but having Derek here causes my sleep patterns to shift. More specifically, I don't sleep as much at night—even though he tries to let me. It's hard to care about rest with him in my bed.

The sounds of him moving around inside drift to me on the sea breeze. He's opening closet doors and looking for any signs of disturbance. It's very comforting, even though I feel silly worrying him so much over a bad dream, which was probably induced by all the preoccupation with my ex.

Further down below us the waves crash against the shoreline. One of the things I love about my new home is how secluded it is from the rest of civilization, but I confess, Derek's current obsession with Sloan's whereabouts has me spooked.

I can't tell him what my nightmare was really about.

Joining me on the side porch, he pulls me close against his chest again. "Nothing seems out of place, but I don't know what all you did while I was gone."

"Just worked, came out here. Then I was tired and took a nap."

I can see him thinking, and I almost jump out of my skin at the very loud and completely unexpected roar of a motorcycle engine. We're both up, but I beat him to the door.

"Why is Patrick on a Harley?"

Derek's lips tighten, and he catches me by the waist, pulling me back and flipping the lock on the door. "Stay here."

Frowning, I watch as he stalks out to meet his partner.

Patrick's royal blue Charger is in my driveway next to Derek's black Audi, and I can only assume they got separated somehow. *But how?* I can't hear what they're saying. Patrick's expression wavers back and forth between irritation and relief, and they talk for a few minutes longer. Then Patrick walks over and straddles the bike once more. He pulls the black helmet over his head and kicks the engine to life. Derek gives him a nod, and with a roar, his partner heads toward town.

Derek turns and heads back to the house. His brow is furrowed, and he studies the ground as he walks. One arm is crossed, and he's holding his bicep, the other hand is a clenched fist.

Stepping back, I let him in the door, but he pauses to flip the metal lock again before taking my hand and leading me into the house.

"I feel like I'm the one out of the loop." The blanket is still clutched over my shoulders as I follow him.

He doesn't answer.

"How did you and Patrick get separated?"

We're in the kitchen now, and I watch as he pulls down an unopened bottle of Scotch. "Patrick invited us over for dinner tonight."

He cracks the seal and pours a small amount into a glass and shoots it back. A little wince creases his eyes, and he puts the glass in the sink.

"I've never seen you drink in the afternoon."

I'm back in his arms, and his face is buried in my hair as he inhales deeply. A warm shiver travels up my arms despite my concern.

"I've never been so worried about you." His voice is low against my neck. "But you're okay now. And I'm here."

I'm unsure how to pursue this. My dream-inspired panic is fresh in my memory, and now he's behaving so strangely. I want to argue. I want to fight this type of existence, to insist this *isn't* how I'm going to live, dammit. I won't be afraid in my own home.

But anxiety is still holding my shoulders tightly. With a sigh, I step back and manage a smile. "If we're having dinner at Elaine's, I want to shower first. We always stay late."

He smiles in response, but it's not as bright as usual. "Not too late. I know you need your rest."

Stretching up on my tiptoes, I kiss his lips. "Thanks." Then I head back to my bedroom to get ready. For the short-term, I'll trust him and put this discussion on hold.

Thursday night always feels like the start of the weekend, even though Friday is still a workday. Elaine stands by the stove, a glass of white wine in her hand when we arrive. The room smells like tomato-ey deliciousness, and my friend is still dressed from school in a navy pencil skirt and a pink sweater-set. She's also barefoot, and her light-blonde hair is pulled up in a messy bun.

"Come in!" She calls, giving the pot one last stir before dropping the wooden spoon and stepping over to hug me. "I hope you're in the mood for Italian. Oh, Mel. You're absolutely glowing!"

She squeezes my arms before smiling up at Derek. "You're now officially my third favorite person on the planet."

He laughs and leans down to kiss her cheek. Her head tilts toward him. "I guess third is better than thirtieth."

"Well, I have to count Patrick first, Melissa second-"

"I've been replaced!"

She laughs, and just then Patrick emerges from the side room, his arms full of laundry. "Hey, guys." The sunshine is back in his voice, and it's very reassuring.

"She's got you doing laundry now?" Shaking my head, I glance up at Derek.

"I've got a service that comes once a week." He almost sounds apologetic, which makes me laugh more.

Patrick pauses to speak low in my ear. "Not all of us are as set as Mr. Alexander."

"Wait!" Elaine stops him and pulls a dress out of the load. "This is dry clean only."

"Sorry, babe, but it's got a little stain on it." He gives her a wink, and she shakes her head.

She doesn't notice that when she pulls out the dress, a gold silk tie goes with it. It hits the floor, and I pick it up, noticing how horribly misshapen and nearly torn it is. "Oh, no!" Flipping it over, I see an Armani label.

Patrick reemerges from the laundry room. "What?"

"Your tie is ruined. What happened to it?"

"Oh!" Elaine charges back and snatches it out of my hand. Her cheeks are flaming red, and Patrick laughs loudly.

"Elaine, tell number two what happened to my best tie." That devilish gleam is in his eye, and it takes me a second to catch up. "My kinky fiancée thought she'd play dominatrix, but I had to set her straight."

"Patrick Knight!" My best friend's voice is a loud command as she returns from dropping both items in their bedroom.

"There she goes again."

Derek coughs a laugh, and my eyebrows fly up. "Well, okay then." I'm trying not to laugh, too. "TMI, number one."

"Good work." Derek gives him a fist bump. I elbow my own fiancé sharply in the stomach. He grunts another laugh. "I mean... sorry about your tie?"

Elaine's voice is high, and her back is turned while she stabs the wooden spoon in the pot repeatedly. "We can all just stop talking about it now!"

"I'm only teasing you, babe." Patrick goes behind her and holds her waist before kissing her neck. "You know I love your little stunts."

I cross to the cabinet and pull down another wine glass. "On that note, we should have drinks. Derek, wine?"

He nods, and I go to the fridge to pull out the bottle of pinot grigio Elaine's having and a root beer. "You got my favorite."

She glances over her shoulder past Patrick. "Yeah, I figured you were getting sick of ginger ale all the time."

Derek takes the wine glass from me and follows Patrick into the living room. They immediately launch into a discussion, but Patrick's speaking so low I can barely hear him.

"I touched base with Toni and assured them we'd be back tomorrow. Gabe wants his bike now, but he'll give me twenty-four hours."

Derek's voice is equally low. "I don't like leaving her while he's still MIA."

Frustrated, I go to where they're talking. "Please tell me what's going on. You know I don't like being in the dark."

Derek's shoulders drop, and Patrick turns to me. "Sloan's gone off the radar. We don't like it in view of what happened in Baltimore. We still don't have answers, and we're not ready."

My brow lines. "Ready for what?"

"We've been working on a plan since the Jessica Black report turned up. Derek was trying to establish a financial connection, but it was going nowhere. Sloan's too experienced at covering his tracks."

I look up at Derek, and he catches my hand. "Patrick's idea could work, but we hadn't started talking about it when my man in Baltimore alerted me that Sloan was missing."

The dream, the memory of feeling like he was there watching me, causes a strange roaring sound to grow in my ears. Shivers fly up my shoulders, and I understand the meaning of Derek's panicked appearance, Patrick's following behind on the motorcycle. "You drove back today because you were afraid—"

"He left me stranded in Raleigh," Patrick tries to laugh it off, but it isn't working. "I had to borrow Lylah's boyfriend's bike, and that is not something those guys do lightly. I had to leave my watch with him."

"Your Tag?"

"I'll get it back."

My eyes move to Derek's, and I can't decide which of the emotions surging through me is stronger—the intense love I feel for him or the intense hatred I feel for my ex.

The noise is pushing against my temples, and I step into the loving arms waiting for me. I hold his waist, and he holds me tightly until my trembling subsides.

"I hate this so much." My voice is barely above a whisper, but he hears me.

His voice is a low vibration in response. "I'm going to fix it. You'll never be afraid again."

Hidden in his arms, inhaling the clean-woodsy scent I love, I find calm. Until finally I'm able to look around again, and I notice how quiet it is in the room. Patrick is back in the kitchen talking to Elaine.

Lifting my chin, Derek smiles before kissing my lips. "I'm not going anywhere if you don't feel safe. You and the baby are my first priority now."

Shaking my head, I push my hair behind my ears, working hard to regain my composure. "I can go to

Mom's office tomorrow and work. I'll be okay. It's like I keep saying, he cannot win. I won't let him."

Elaine calls from the kitchen. "Feel like eating something?"

Touching his rough cheek, I nod. "Let's have dinner. You and Patrick keep your plans for tomorrow."

His lips press into a smile, and he takes my hand in his, kissing the backs of my fingers before walking with me to the table. Elaine smiles and steps around to squeeze my shoulders. "If you ever want to hang out with me at school, I can always use an extra set of hands."

"Thanks." I pat her back. "I think I'll spend the afternoon with Mom tomorrow, but I'll keep your offer just in case."

"We'll have the information we need by tomorrow, I expect." Patrick joins us at the table. "Then it'll just be a matter of timing. We can plan it all out from here, where we can keep an eye on you."

He winks at me, but when Derek speaks, his voice is serious. "I appreciate you watching her for me these past weeks."

Shaking out my napkin and putting it in my lap, I pretend to be offended. "All this time, I thought you kept inviting me over because you enjoyed my company."

Elaine passes the basket of bread. "You've been eating us out of house and home. Jeez! I'm glad Derek's finally here."

"I have not!"

She bursts out laughing. "I was only teasing! But I want some beachside dinners at your place now."

"You got it. I love having you guys over."

The rest of dinner conversation is devoted to easy subjects—the weather, Patrick's newfound desire to own a Harley, Elaine's loud protests over the dangers of motorcycles. It's not very late when we call it a night, and as we say our goodbyes, I catch Patrick's arm, pulling him aside. Derek and Elaine continue talking.

"Thank you for watching over me."

He smiles and shrugs. "I promised Derek. Besides, it wasn't any more than he'd have done for me."

My eyes narrow. "You say that, but I know better. I also won't hear anything bad about you ever again. Everybody'd better look out."

"That might be hard. There's plenty of bad about me that's true."

"Not for me. It's all good now." He breathes a chuckle, but I'm not through. "Would you promise me something this time?"

Golden-hazel eyes meet mine. "What?"

"Promise you'll look after him now. For me." I touch his arm. "Don't let him do anything..." *What's the right way to say it?* "Anything that could mean he'll be taken away from me?"

His warm hand covers mine. "You mean anything illegal or potentially deadly?"

"Exactly."

"I promise. I've got his back." Patrick isn't smiling, and I know I can trust him. He means what he says.

Derek's with us, and we drop the subject, acting casual, like we were just discussing how to get Elaine onboard the Harley train.

My fiancé takes my hand, pausing before we go out the door. "I'll meet you at ten. We should be there by noon to wrap this up and make a plan."

"See you in the morning."

The cottage is dark and quiet when we arrive. Derek stops in the kitchen to check his messages, but I go straight through the house, flipping on lights, refusing to be timid in my own place.

I go to the bathroom and switch on the hot water. An oversized, jetted bathtub is one of the perks of living in an intended vacation residence, and tonight my whole body craves the comfort of a steaming, swirling bubble bath.

Digging under the cabinet, I find the jar of foaming bath salts I bought at the spa in Scottsdale and add several scoops to the stream rushing from the faucet. Once the temperature is right and the bubbles have risen, I strip out of all my clothes, tie up my hair and slide down into the cactus-flower-scented jets.

The water is the perfect level of hotness. My head rests on a foam pillow attached to the side, and I close my eyes, allowing the swirling water to soothe away the night. I don't realize I'm asleep until the soft press of Derek's lips against my forehead followed by the light scruff of his beard against my brow wakes me. My eyes flutter open, and he smiles down, fully dressed and leaning over the tub.

"Tired?" His voice is gentle.

Nodding, I lift one hand out of the now-warm water and touch his cheek. "Join me?"

I watch as he unbuttons his sleeve and rolls it up to his elbow. One hand on the wall behind my head, he leans forward and captures my lips as his other hand slides beneath the foam to cup my breast.

A breathy moan slips from my mouth into his, and keeping my eyes closed, I cover his hand with mine, following his movements from one breast to the other, his thumb slowly circling my hardening nipples.

He leans up and our eyes meet. "Good news." My eyebrows rise with curiosity, and he continues. "Sloan's back on the radar. He's in Charleston. Bennett's watching him and promises to keep me updated."

"Now you don't have to worry." My voice is thick from napping followed by all the steamy kisses and touches. "I can stay home and work tomorrow."

"I'd still like it if you had someone with you." His voice is soft with a touch of sexy, fanning the heat he's aroused in me.

"*I'd* like it if you were less clothed and in here while we discuss it."

"I'm not sure we'll do much discussing that way."

Sitting forward in the tub, I carefully unfasten his buttons with the tips of my fingers until his olive chest is revealed. A scattering of dark hair covers the top of his lined torso, and I chew my bottom lip remembering how it feels against my breasts. With the pad of his thumb, he touches my mouth.

"Don't bite your lip." He leans in and brushes his against mine. "Let me do that."

He gives me a little nibble, and I'm coming undone. "You're taking too long."

In a flash he stands, pushes his dark jeans down his hips, taking his boxer briefs with them. My breath catches at the sight of his gorgeous body nude in front of me. He's fully erect as he steps in and slides beneath the foam at the opposite end of the tub.

"Mmm... warm." Large hands slide to my waist, pulling me onto his lap as he leans back in the water. I'm already slick, so it doesn't take much. I reach around behind me and guide his tip into my throbbing opening. We both sigh as he rocks deep into me.

I lean forward, holding the tub on each side of his head while his mouth covers my breast, sucking a tight nipple.

—

A loud moan from me, and he moves up, his voice cracking in my ear. "We'll probably get water everywhere."

The sound of his growing desire sparks mine even hotter. "That's what towels are for."

His lips consume my words, his tongue sweeping in to find mine, and his hands grip my ass beneath the surface. Holding my body still, his hips rock into mine. Our mouths break away with a groan, and the water is swaying with us, splashing over the side. His mouth is at my shoulder, and he gives me another little bite. I tremble, holding him as his thrusting increases in speed and depth.

My orgasm mounts, and I feel my brow tense in ecstasy as he moves. The tightness below my navel becomes unbearable until at last it breaks, leaving me crying out his name. His movements don't slow, and I clutch his shoulders. The sound of me coming seems to push him over, and after a few final thrusts, he groans low, shooting off deep between my quivering thighs.

His hips move slower, and I kiss him along his rough jaw. My body is so relaxed and satisfied. I make my way to his ear, whispering my love for him as his arms wrap tightly around my waist. He kisses my neck, moving his hands out of the water to cup my cheeks, bringing my face so our eyes are level.

"Nothing is going to take you away from me." His blue eyes are intense, and his brow lowered.

Nodding, I lift my own hands out of the water, lightly holding his neck, my thumbs at the corners of his mouth. "Nothing."

An inhale, and he pulls me against him, my cheek at his forehead, his face against my chest. For several moments we hold each other, until I notice the water is growing cold.

Lifting my head and sliding back down to kiss his nose, I smile. "Let's move this party to the bed, okay?"

A sexy grin spreads across his lips. "I'll have to get used to being with you longer than three days. We don't have to be so urgent, trying to make the most of every moment."

"Hmm." I can't help a frown. "I'm not sure I like the sound of that."

"You won't always be the 'horny pregnant lady,' as you like to say. I'm sure you'll appreciate me pacing myself."

My lips poke out as I consider this suggestion. Then my eyes roam from his thick dark waves tipped with bath water, hanging sexy in his blue eyes, his scruffy beard and full lips hiding straight white teeth. His amazing body...

"I think we should just play this whole 'pacing ourselves' thing by ear."

He laughs and pulls me against him, rolling us in the tub so that we're chest to chest, our bodies touching from head to toe under the water. I shriek and laugh, loving his possessiveness.

"*Nobody*. Is taking you away from me." He emphasizes the words softly before covering my lips again with his.

Chasing his kisses, laughing as happiness radiates through my core, it's hard for me to ever imagine having enough of him. But I wiggle, struggling to free myself from his vice grip. At once, he releases me.

"We're going to catch a chill if we don't get out of this tub. Not to mention turning into prunes." Standing, I reach for a fluffy white towel as his hands slide up my leg. He sits up and kisses the side of my thigh.

I reach back and slide my hand through is hair before stepping out. "Come on."

The grin on his face as he watches me dry myself tightens my stomach. His expression is a mixture of raw desire and pure appreciation. And love. Always love.

I can't help feeling a little self-conscious about my new figure as I drop a few towels around the tub to soak up the spilled water. "Meet you in the bedroom."

I head down the hall, hurrying to my dresser. I have something red and lacy in mind, something I know is Derek's favorite, but I pause in front of my mirror, my eyes searching my neck in the reflection.

A flash of panic hits me, and I quickly feel all around the dresser top. I don't know how I didn't notice before. The excitement I was just feeling is gone, and I grasp my neck. *Where is it?*

Running back to the bathroom, the towel still tied under my arms, I pass him headed in my direction.

He steps back against the wall. "Melissa?"

Confusion is in his voice, but I can only think one thing. "No!" I cry, plunging my hands into the receding water and feeling around frantically.

I can't find it. I sit back on my heels watching the water disappear. "No no *NO*!!!" Diving forward, I plunge both my hands in the half-inch left, frantically sweeping dying bubbles aside, feeling all over the bottom of the large tub.

Derek grasps my upper arms. "Mel, you're scaring me. What's wrong?"

"It's not here." My throat is so tight, I almost can't speak the words. Jumping up, I run to the kitchen, my eyes sweeping every inch of the floor as I go.

My bag is sitting on the counter, and I grab it, flip it over and dump the contents all over the bar. Lipstick, wallet, keys, pens, peppermint, loose change, dental floss…

I sweep my fingers through it all, desperate. "No!" I whisper, my voice cracking with tears.

Derek's right with me as I run out to the side porch, flipping on the light. So much adrenaline is pulsing through me, I don't even notice the cold. Shoving my hands into the cushions, I grasp and feel...

Nothing. *Nothing...*

It's not there.

"Oh, god!" I collapse against the small couch, a flood of tears streaming down my cheeks. "I've lost it... I've lost it."

"What, baby?" Derek's voice cracks now. "What have you lost?"

"Your necklace..." A sob hiccups in my throat, momentarily stealing my words. "Your heart... I lost it. Oh god..."

More tears soak my cheeks, and he pulls me against his chest. We're both sitting cross-legged in towels on the floor of my screened-in side porch. It's freezing, but I can't tell if I'm shaking from the cold or the heartbreak.

One large hand holds my waist, the other smooths my back, but even Derek's massive strength can salvage what's happened.

I lean back to look at him, but I can't speak. The shivering and crying have stolen my words.

I can tell he's lost. His brow creases with helplessness. "But... It wasn't really my heart. It was just a symbol—"

Shaking my head, my chin drops. "No. You gave it to me. It was the first thing you ever gave me, and I loved it so much." Tears are streaming down my face. I can't stop them.

I'm on the verge of ugly crying, and I don't even care. That little necklace was more precious to me than the most expensive piece of jewelry I might ever get in my life, and now it's gone.

"Melissa. Stop. Look at me." He lifts my chin and pulls my face close to his, kissing the tears on my cheeks. "My heart is here, with you. You always have my heart, even without a symbol. I'm always yours."

I slip my arm around his neck, burying my face against his shoulder, and he gathers me to his chest and stands, holding me. For the briefest second, I wonder at his ability to do that so easily. Then my memory floods as he walks us back to the bedroom and fresh tears come.

"You're so tired." His voice is quiet and soothing as he places me on the bed, pulling back the blankets. "We'll look for it tomorrow. It'll turn up. I promise."

I want to believe that, but somehow, I'm certain it's gone.

Untying the towel still under my arms, he removes it then lifts my legs and puts them between the sheets. We're both naked when he slides in beside me. Hugging me close, he strokes the top of my arm slowly.

"Just rest, and trust me. We'll find that necklace." His voice is warm and comforting, and I must be more tired than I realized. Or the sadness has taken my strength.

Either way, it's not long before my heavy limbs relax, and I succumb to sleep.

CHAPTER 7: PATRICK'S PROPOSAL
DEREK

Only a few times in my life have I felt completely helpless, and the top two occurred in the last twenty-four hours. Watching Mel fall apart last night was almost as bad as that fucking drive from Raleigh. Holding her now as she sleeps, I think about what happened.

As if dealing with Sloan isn't enough, she's completely undone over a necklace, a trinket that cost me less than two hundred dollars. You'd think it was made of pure platinum encrusted with diamonds.

If I remember correctly, she threatened to throw it in the ocean once when she was angry with me. Now it's more valuable than what we thought was hidden in Al Capone's empty vault, and I can't console her.

At the same time, I adore her so much for it.

The fact that such a small thing, the only thing I could find that late night in Scottsdale to give her — the night when she'd first wanted to tell me she loved me but couldn't. I'd wanted to tell her I loved her, too...

It *had* been pretty important that night to do something to mark the moment. Everything in me demanded I make her mine forever, but I knew what we had in the desert was tentative. We hoped for so much more, but we couldn't have it then. I didn't know if I'd ever see her again, yet she'd stolen my heart. That necklace was the only thing I could give her to make it real.

With a deep exhale, I accept what she's feeling right now over losing it. It's pretty heartbreaking, and as much as I mean it when I say it doesn't matter, I know how sentimental that delicate piece of 24-karat gold is.

It'll turn up. I reassure myself as much as her. And dammit, if it doesn't, I'll fucking buy her another one. Maybe the new one *will* be platinum encrusted with diamonds. I can even have it delivered with the original message.

She stirs, and I hold her closer. She's upset, but asleep, she looks peaceful. I want her to feel calm and not worry.

Her blue eyes blink open, and her voice is a soft whisper. "Hi."

The familiar squeeze of love hits me right in the stomach, and I never want it to ease, no matter how many years we pass sharing the same bed. No pacing ourselves, only love, as much and as often as we want it.

"Feeling better?" I smooth my palm over her forehead, back into her hair, but her soft lips press together.

"Not really."

I roll forward and kiss that ivory forehead, right where my hand just was. "I'm sorry I have to leave with

Patrick today, otherwise I'd stay here and tear the house apart until I found it."

"It's okay." She pushes me onto my back, resting her cheek on my chest, hugging my torso. "I know this job is important, and I don't mind searching by myself. It'll probably be easier because I know where all I've been."

My phone buzzes, and I glance at the clock. "I've got to get moving, or I'll be late meeting Patrick."

We both sit up, and she wraps the sheet under her arms as her eyes travel around the room, scanning all the baseboards. I know she'll do it—the whole day, searching.

Cupping her jaw, I kiss her lips lightly. "Try not to worry. I'll make it right. No matter what."

Her eyes flicker to mine and she manages a little smile. "Be safe today."

Melissa is on my mind the entire drive to Raleigh. I want to be there with her and make sure she's not sad, or worse, crying again. Patrick's ahead of me on the borrowed bike, and I follow him off the Interstate in the direction of the seedy bar.

Once we're in the parking lot, he slows down and motions for me to find a spot while he manages the bike. I meet up with him heading into the Skinniflute, but he holds my arm before we enter.

"When we meet with Toni this time, hang back. Let me take the lead." His brow is tense, and I notice his jaw flex. "She wasn't too thrilled about working with you."

Glancing away, I exhale a laugh. "That makes two of us. Sloan Reynolds is used to high-class action, not part-time hookers."

My partner releases my arm and jerks the metal door open. "She cleans up well, and she owes me a favor. Just let me handle it."

Following my abrupt departure yesterday, Patrick set up a meeting when she wasn't on the clock. As a result, Toni Durango is sitting in the same wooden booth waiting when we enter the dive.

As directed, I hang back while Patrick strides over, smiling that cocky grin of his. "Thanks for meeting up with us today."

A cup of coffee is in front of her, and she sits up, leaning forward over the table. "What I wouldn't give for a cigarette."

"You quit?" He slides in next to her, and I take my place across the table, hands on the bench at my sides.

"For the fiftieth time. I don't expect it to stick." She has the voice of a smoker, low and husky.

I try to picture her "cleaned up" as Patrick put it. Today, she's wearing thick black eyeliner, fake lashes, and velvet red lipstick. Her black hair is pulled back in a ponytail, and I fully expect to find tattoo sleeves if the leopard-print cardigan she's wearing over her black tank comes off.

Sloan will *not* go for this.

Her brown eyes meet mine. "Patrick said the reason you ran off yesterday was about this guy."

Sliding a glance at my partner, he's still wearing his lady-killer grin, but his eyes are telling me to take it easy. Like this is my first job.

"He's an abusive asshole, and I suspect a murderer. My concern is he's coming after my fiancée, who happens to be his ex-wife."

This girl has either seen a lot of shit or she's used to handling it, because her expression never falters.

Her lips press together then, and her eyes narrow. "They always come back. You think they're gone, the law is on your side, but there's no stopping those

90

motherfuckers." Her hands tighten around the mug in front of her. "The only good abuser is a dead abuser."

"Sounds like you have experience with guys like this."

"Not me." She shakes her head and looks down. "My step-sister was shot by her ex before they finally put him away. Lylah's aunt was almost beat to death... If there's one kind of trouble I *do* avoid, it's creeps like that."

Patrick leans forward as if on cue. "He's into sex for hire. Our plan was to set the guy up. Use you as sort-of... bait."

"We'll be there the whole time," I add. "You wouldn't be alone with him ever."

She blinks down to the table. "What's in it for me?"

As much as I'm sure we have nothing in common, I'm on her side this time. I wouldn't ask any woman to play prostitute — even ones with experience, and I'm about to call the whole thing off when Patrick cuts in.

"Five thousand dollars, immunity... and knowing you helped get a killer off the streets."

Poker face or not, I saw her eyes spark at the mention of money. We didn't discuss it, but I'm slick with his proposal. I'd gladly pay any amount for the peace of mind Melissa and I will gain knowing this guy is dealt with.

She studies the coffee cup as she appears to be turning the prospect over in her mind. "Why can't you get him yourself? Without me?"

I answer this one. "He's not your average, run of the mill lowlife. He's connected. He's got money, power, and lawyers who can get him out of anything."

"Escorts," Patrick adds. "He uses *escorts*."

Straightening her arms out in front of her, she examines her fingernails. "In that case, I'll need some of that money up front. Mani-Pedi, hair, body makeup to cover the tats…"

"What tats?" Patrick's brow creases, and she smiles like he's so naïve.

We both watch as she removes her sweater, and just as I suspected. Sleeves.

"Well fuck me." He laughs. "I had no idea."

She laughs, too. "I did fuck you. It was pretty fucking hot."

"Okay." That's the last thing I'm interested in hearing about. Their whole connection still pisses me off. "We can give you a thousand up front. Do the works. Hair, wardrobe—"

"I know my job." Her eyes flash at me, and her voice is sharp.

I put a lid on it. Patrick's right. She responds better to him.

"This guy prefers wavy, light brown hair." He reaches inside the leather bike jacket he's wearing and pulls out a folded sheet of paper. "Something like this."

When he puts the sheet on the table, smoothing it open, you would've thought it was on fire. Toni jumps back then she stands quickly out of the booth, snatching up the page.

"What… Where did you get this?" She seems panicky now, and Patrick's out of the booth just as fast.

"It's the Baltimore police report. It's who we think is his last victim. It's what put Derek on the alert."

"No." She's shaking her head, and I can see her eyes flying down the page as she reads. "No…"

The first indication she's crying are the lines. It's like an invisible hand draws two black stripes down each of her cheeks from the outer corners of her eyes to her chin.

She straightens up and spins on a mile-high heel, headed for the bar. "Lylah!"

The younger girl pops up at once. "What's wrong?" She passes over napkins, waiting for a response.

"I need a cigarette." One of the regulars, hunched over his lunch stretches out a soft pack of Reds, and Toni takes one. Her hands are trembling as she lights up and pulls in a deep drag.

Patrick and I exchange a glance before we follow her over to the bar, where she's now dabbing her eyes with the small napkins.

"And a whiskey."

Lylah is quick to set her up.

We're all waiting for an explanation, but we don't get it until after she's shot the brown liquid and glanced at the paper once more. Her voice is husky. "He killed her?"

Carefully, I answer. "I'm almost certain he did."

Patrick puts a hand on her shoulder. "Did you know Jessica Black?"

She pushes a bitter laugh through her lips and shakes her head no. "When I knew her, she was Tiffany Cedric. She was just a kid working in Myrtle Beach, thinking she could pick up some cash as an escort. An *escort*, as you say." She takes another long drag and taps the shot glass. Lylah's quick to hook her up. "She wanted me to show her the ropes. Thought she'd put herself through college and then walk away."

She sips the second shot then slowly turns and carries it back to the booth where we started. Patrick and I follow.

Toni's shoulders are hunched as she slides into the seat. This time Patrick is on the outside. "When's the last time you talked to her?"

She sniffs and pours the remainder of the whiskey into the thick, white mug. "Don't remember... more than a year ago. She was so proud she got in at State, a scholarship even. But it wasn't enough. She couldn't pay all her bills."

Patrick's brow is lined, and I know he's trying as cautiously as possible to see if there's anything here we can use. "Is that all you know?"

She circles the mug with a finger, holding her cigarette away from the table. "I got arrested in Myrtle Beach and moved back here. We lost touch, but one of the other girls kept up with her. Last I heard she'd met a daddy."

I'm not certain I understand. "A daddy?"

"A sugar daddy, a rich old guy. They said Tiffany followed him wherever he went." Her voice drops. "They said he liked it rough—bondage, strangling..." She takes another deep drag and exhales the blue smoke. "I guess she liked it that way, too."

For a few moments, we're quiet. Toni's studying the sheet; I expect she's thinking about her dead friend. I'm thinking about how betrayed Melissa felt when she discovered her husband was cheating. I wonder if she knows the extent of his private practices.

Toni breaks our reverie, and her voice has a hard edge that I confess is pretty powerful. "I'll do your fucking job. I'll help you get the fucker who hurt her."

"We'll need to work out a timeline." Patrick is focused, in closer-mode. "He's not in Baltimore at the moment—"

"Probably looking for a new girl." It's a bitter retort, and I can tell Toni's going to do a good job for us. She's got a dog in this fight now. Just like me.

Patrick continues. "When he gets back to Baltimore, we'll work out a chance encounter. Maybe you can meet him at a bar."

Reaching into his jacket a second time, my partner takes out a white, business-sized envelope that's thick with bills. He pulls out ten Benjis and slides them across the table. "You'll get the rest when we settle up."

She picks up the money and folds it, slipping it into her bra. Classy. "You have my number."

And just like that. The plan to capture Sloan is set in motion.

Patrick drops me off at Melissa's beach cottage, and we discuss heading back to Baltimore for the next— however long it takes. On the road I'd gotten confirmation that Sloan is back in Maryland. It's time for us to act, but we need to scout out a secure hotel for Toni that's inconspicuous and somewhat high-end. We also need to be able to be in the next room or somehow in close proximity to where she'll be.

"I'll look for two extra rooms wherever we put Toni," he says. "Will Melissa come with you?"

"No." I'm standing outside the car, talking to him through the window. "I don't want her there, and I'm sure she doesn't want to be there."

"You might run that past her before deciding." He looks out the windshield, away from me. "Melissa's tough. She might surprise you with what she wants."

"She wants to put all of this behind her, and as much as I hate leaving her here alone, at least her mother and Elaine are nearby. We'll be watching Sloan."

He glances back. "Elaine might be with me."

That's not what I want to hear. "What about school?"

Patrick laughs, shaking his head. "She won't admit it, but she doesn't like me working with Toni."

"I can't say I like it myself, but if she helps us, I can overlook a lot." For a moment, I consider assuring Elaine I'll keep an eye on my partner, but I know it's not necessary. Elaine's got him tied up in more ways than one.

"If she decides to stay, I'll ask if she'll bunk in with Mel while we're gone."

Nodding, I pat the top of the car. "Will you be ready tomorrow, noon?"

"With bells on."

He takes off, and I walk slowly toward the little cottage. It's the only residence for several hundred feet, secluded in the sea grass, far enough away from the water that storms aren't a problem, but close enough to run down and enjoy the surf easily.

It's a great place. The only thing I hate about it is she's completely alone out here, and no one is close enough to check on her. The thought twists a sick feeling in my gut.

Through the screen, I can see her sleeping on the small couch on the side porch again, but this time the side door is locked. Somewhat relieved, I pull out the key she gave me and unlock it. She doesn't stir as I cross the small space to where she's curled up on the pillows.

Dropping to my knees, I smooth her hair off her cheek and give her a light kiss there. She's such a heavy sleeper now. Still, a little smile plays at the corner of her mouth.

"Melissa," I whisper, running my thumb across her cheek. I hate to wake her, but it's after six. Kissing her cheek again, I whisper in her ear. "Wake up, beautiful."

She inhales quickly and pulls back, eyes flying open. "Oh!"

"I'm sorry, did I scare you?"

Covering her face with her hand, she laughs. "I was dreaming… about you."

That sounds promising. "Something dirty?"

Her hand lowers, and she gives me those eyes. "So judgmental. I would never call what we do dirty."

Grinning, I wrap her in my arms. "Now I feel challenged. How can I change your mind about this?"

Her elbows are bent, and she's threading her fingers in my hair still smiling. "Whatever we do, I won't be able to call it dirty. I love you too much."

There's no getting around it. She gets a kiss for that, but just as I push her lips apart, tasting her sweet mouth, finding her tongue, she puts her hands on my cheeks and moves me back.

"Tell me about today. Were you and Patrick successful? Everything work out?"

Remembering how today went, what we learned about Jessica Black and what's coming provokes a frown I can't hide. Melissa is on it fast. "Did she not agree to help you?"

"She agreed to help us." Releasing her, I rise from my knees to sit on the end of the couch, pulling her feet in my lap. "And I'm more convinced than ever we're doing the right thing. Even if it bends a few rules."

"Sloan's built his life around bending rules and deception."

I'm surprised by this response from her. "So you're not against what we're doing anymore?"

She sighs and pushes herself up to a sitting position. "The more I've thought about it, the more convinced I am that even if he leaves me alone, he'll just find a new victim. How can I let that happen?"

I unwrap the blanket and find one of her soft feet. Massaging it, I nod my agreement. She had to come to this decision on her own, and I'm glad she did.

"He *would* find another victim, it seems. Based on what Toni told us today."

Melissa's eyes drift to the screen facing the ocean and beyond it. "He was so charming in the beginning. Kind and generous."

"You never told me how you fell in love with him, but I assumed he had to be different."

She looks back at her lap, and I know this is hard for her. She once told me what happened with Sloan was her "humiliating truth." I want her to know she can trust me with this. I would never judge her. Her small foot is still in my hand, and I give her arch a deep rub.

"That feels good." She gives me a small smile, and I return it. "He reminded me of my dad a little. Not in a creepy way. But my father was much older than my mom. I'm sure they had a passionate relationship, but all I saw growing up was how he took care of her. How she would go to him for advice, and how good he was to her."

"You said Sloan was one of your clients."

"His father was. Actually, it was the family business, so I interacted with Mr. Reynolds, Sloan, and other executives there. Sloan's father was probably what clouded my judgment. I saw him treat Sloan's mother —"

"He treated her like your father treated your mother, and you assumed like father, like son. It's perfectly reasonable."

Her eyes are full of gratitude when they meet mine. "It felt so familiar and good. Until it didn't."

I fish out her other foot to rub. "Don't want you walking funny the rest of the day."

"Unless it's from sleeping with you?"

It's hard to ignore the stirring below my belt when she makes suggestions like that. "I think you have a type, darling. You like older men."

She pulls her foot back and crawls across the sofa into my arms. "You're only a little older —"

"Ten years."

"Compared to twenty." Her arms are around my neck, but she drops her chin. "I was such a dumb little girl when I met him."

"You were twenty —"

"Six. Almost twenty-seven and completely swept off my small-town feet by his wealth and sophistication."

Catching that chin, I lift her face to kiss it. Her skin is so soft. "We all make mistakes every now and then." I think about the brief period I knew Sloan years ago. "He did my orientation when I started at Princeton, so we spent a little time together. I never saw any sign of his true character."

My lips move from her cheek to her temple, to her hair, where I inhale deeply. Something is definitely on the rise down below, aided by her hand finding its way under my shirt and sliding across my stomach.

"That was a mistake." Her voice is thick with desire. "You were a surprise. A gift."

Speaking of gifts, I notice one gift is still not around her neck, but I'm not about to spoil this moment. "I hope you were able to relax today."

Her head drops to my shoulder, and I kiss her again, noticing that wandering hand is unfastening the button of my jeans. An ache moves through my groin, anticipating her touch.

"You must think I'm terribly lazy always being asleep when you get here." Her hand is inside my jeans now, small fingers wrapping around me, sliding slowly up and down.

My voice is a husky groan in her ear before I kiss it. "I'd never call you lazy." I pull her up, so I can attend to the skin around her neck. She shivers in that delicious way as I consume her.

"Every day at three, just like clockwork, I'm falling asleep." She gasps as my hand travels under her sweater, pushing her bra aside so I can caress her breast. "I've never done that before."

"It's the baby." Moving her completely onto my lap in a straddle, I push her sweater and bra all the way up, pulling her breasts together and taking them in my mouth. Her head drops to mine with a moan.

My dick rises out of my pants, but I'm not sure if she's ready until I notice her grasping at the hem of her skirt, pulling it up quickly. She's on her knees in front of me, and in one quick movement, she shoves her panties to the side and drops hard and fast on my aching cock.

"Fuck!" I can't help groaning it feels so good. My hips are pushing into her, and she's riding, both hands against the wall behind my head.

"Oh, god!" She's riding hard and I'm pushing fast, fueled by the gripping and pulling of her inner muscles.

I'm about to blow, and I grab her waist, moving her up and down, my thumb circling her clit.

"Oh, Derek!" She cries out, and I lose it. It seems my timing wasn't far off because her knees clutch my waist, and she's holding onto me, moaning in my ear. I only lightly touch her ass now, letting her ride it out, not wanting to disturb her pleasure. It's fucking sending me to the moon, and I drop my head back, savoring the sensations of her coming over me.

A few movements more, we hold each other for a bit, coming down. God, to think I have a lifetime of this to look forward to. She falls forward, smiling contentedly.

"Nothing about that is dirty." Her hands go to my cheeks, and she kisses all around my mouth. "It's pure... and real... and gorgeous... and fucking hot."

I'm still inside her as she moves around, and damn if her sexy mouth isn't about to have me ready to go again. "You won't catch me trying to change your mind."

A small laugh, a little nibble, and I have to carry her inside for more.

Chapter 8: No Ghosts
Melissa

For once I'm awake before Derek. This silly pregnancy is about to drive me crazy with all the exhaustion and the weight gain and the hormones, and now this morning I can't sleep.

Okay, the hormones aren't so bad. If we hadn't started out sharing some pretty hot moments, I'd say we were setting the bar on being insatiable teenagers. A little laugh pushes through my throat as I lie on my side watching him sleep. He's so gorgeous, and I won't lie, this surge of protectiveness he's displaying is incredibly sexy.

I've managed to wiggle out of his embrace—it always takes me forever to get used to sleeping alone after he's been here. He holds me so close against him all night. Now I'm facing him, studying his relaxed profile, small nose, full lips. The first flecks of grey are appearing in his dark beard. It's so few, I can almost count them, and they make him even more attractive in my eyes.

Lifting my hand quietly so I don't wake him, I lightly move a dark wave off his eyes. He'll start complaining about needing a haircut if he stays with me much longer. Just then his violet-blue eyes blink open, and my insides flood with the most amazing sensation— my friend, my lover, my savior... the father of my child.

"I love you," I whisper.

He leans forward to kiss my forehead before pushing up on his elbow to reach the bottle of water on his nightstand. "You're awake early."

I span his large bicep with my hand. "You haven't been working out as much."

His head ducks with a laugh. "Are you saying I'm out of shape?"

"Of course not!" I dive into him. "You're perfect! I just... I don't want you to be unhappy spending so much time with me. I'm messing up your routine."

His arms go around me, and I'm propped on his chest, looking into his eyes. "Darling, I'd give up any routine to have this time with you."

"I love it when your New Orleans comes out."

"I have another thing that would like to come out."

"Is that so?" Scooting my hips in line with his, I slide myself down, onto his morning wood. His head drops back and his eyes close with a groan.

Nibbling the base of his neck, my voice is thick now. "I can take care of that situation."

Minutes later, we're panting and sweaty and so satisfied...

Except I'm hungry.

I'm on my back now, and he's kissing the line of my collarbone as I think. "Remember that place that didn't have the Applewood smoked bacon?"

He chuckles, still inside me. "The Sawmill?"

"You have a very good memory. Much better than mine these days." I push against his shoulder and he rolls back. "Give me a second to get cleaned up, and we can go get some breakfast."

Hopping out of the bed, I skip over to the bathroom. He's lying on his side, elbow bent, head resting on his hand, and I can't help it. I run back over to kiss his lips, but I scoot away before he can catch me again. We'll never leave the bedroom if that happens.

"I think you're starting to show," he calls after me.

I stop before getting in the shower and turn to the side, looking in the mirror. I think he's right. Finally, my stomach is starting to round out a bit. Smoothing my hands over the small bump, I'm so happy.

"You're right," I call back, before stepping into the stall.

In no time, I'm showered and fresh, and we're heading out the door to the old restaurant designed to look like a lumberjack's shop. Tools of the trade hang on the wood-paneled walls, and the menus have pictures of all the selections in them.

"I know you appreciate our fine dining options here." I can't help teasing his refined palate. "But I truly love their breakfast."

A waitress appears. She's in her fifties, and her hair's piled in a bun on her head.

"Hey, Melissa. Haven't seen you in a while." She smacks gum as she waits for our order—no notepad required.

"Hi, Peg!" My voice is cheerful. I've known her since I was a teenager.

Derek scans the laminated menu. "I'll have a Sawmill Eggs Benedict. Gravy is my favorite hollandaise."

Giggling, I scan over all the selections. "I want eggs every way. And regular coffee... just this once."

He shrugs. "I can't tell you no."

Peg nods and then shakes her head. We're sitting on the same side of the booth, which I know is so silly and young-loverish, but I can't help it. I don't know if it's hormones or what, but the situation with Sloan, losing my necklace, none of it seems to dampen how I'm feeling this morning.

Scooting closer to him, I slide the dark hair away from his face as he sips his coffee. "I love having you with me longer than two days at a time."

He puts the cup down and stretches an arm around my shoulders. "We really need to find a compromise solution to our home-base situation."

Our blue eyes meet, and I can't help kissing him. "Then stop fighting me and move here."

"Melissa..." he groans.

I sit back, crossing my arms. "What's wrong with Wilmington?"

"Other than the fact there's not a decent airport for miles, it's cut off from everything—"

"Like living in Paradise. A dream..."

"For a serial killer. Or any other criminal or societal dropout hoping to escape the long arm of the law."

"You've been working in justice too long."

"I've been very happy Patrick's here to watch over you for me, but I agree with you." He lifts my long, dark hair and kisses my cheek. "Being with you even one extra day is so good. I want us to decide now."

Why did I bring this subject up? I know it's the one thing we can't agree on, and it's also the one thing that could kill my mood. Luckily, the busboys show up at that perfect moment with all our food. Peg's hanging behind them, making sure they deliver the dishes correctly.

"He's having the Sawmill B, she's having all the rest."

I can't help laughing as they unload four plates of eggs prepared in a variety of ways for me to sample. "And my bacon!" A plate of bacon appears in front of me.

"Can I get y'all anything else?" Peg waits chewing her gum, unimpressed.

"We're good, thanks!" I say brightly, and she disappears.

I allow our impasse to give way to the lusciousness of home-cooked breakfast, and we dig in, touching each other every so often as we eat.

"I want to walk on the beach after this," I manage to say around a bite of bacon and eggs.

He nods. "We'll need it." But then his expression turns serious. "I didn't want to tell you this last night, but Patrick and I need to get on the road for Baltimore by noon."

And just like that, my happy mood is gone. Disappeared. He's leaving me in... my eyes wander to the enormous clock hanging in the center of the back wall... two hours.

My chin drops, and his arms are around me just as fast. "I'm sorry." His breath is against my neck, and it's almost torture knowing all of this will be over so soon and for who knows how long this time.

"This is part of the plan?" I hear the highness of my voice, the crack as I say the words. It's pitiful and pathetic, and I don't care.

He inhales deeply and leans back, concern all over his face. "It is. And I think this time it's going to work. I'm going to make sure it does, or I promise — "

107

"Where are you staying? You don't have a place in Baltimore." I won't let him finish what he was trying to say. I also know Patrick won't let him finish it—we've discussed the fact that neither of us will let Derek risk his reputation or his future on someone as worthless as Sloan.

"Patrick started looking for a place last night. I'm sure he's found something nice."

Sadness weighs so heavy on my shoulders, I'm no longer hungry. "Let's get out of here. I want that walk on the beach with you."

He nods and fishes out his wallet. Dropping three twenties on the table, he takes my hand and pulls me out of the booth.

I try to protest. "I'm sure that's way too much—"

"Peg's an old friend of yours?" I nod, and he continues. "We'll give her a special tip then."

Moments later, we're on my beautiful beach. It's cold, and I'm enveloped in fleece, hanging on his arm as the waves pound against the shore. It's windy, and my hair pushes hard away from my face.

"Yesterday, I told you about Sloan." I pull him down to sit beside me on the cool sand. "Tell me about Allison."

His expression changes, and for a moment I think he's going to find that one thing he'll say No to me on. But he doesn't. "Why?"

Shrugging, my hands are in my lap. "I love you. It's an enormous part of your history..." I look out at the waves. The white breakers hit the sand with such force, spray shoots straight up into the wind before it's whipped back out toward the ocean. "Whenever I visit your place, and there are no mementos of your life together, I can't help wondering why."

"I put the pictures away when she died. I guess I've never thought about taking them out again."

"How did you meet her?"

He looks down then puts an arm around my shoulders, drawing me closer to him. "We went to high school together."

A knot forms in my throat. It's silly to feel insecure about a memory, but I need to know his past. "Did you date in high school?

He nods. "She waited for me when I did my first tour in the Gulf. The war broke out, and they all tied the yellow ribbons around the trees..."

"I'm so sorry." Bringing up the subject suddenly feels like the stupidest idea I've ever had. "We don't have to talk about it."

But he catches my face and turns it back to his. "Hey," his voice is a whisper. "I can talk about her with you. I never could with anyone else, but with you it's different."

"How?" I'm wondering if he can ever love me as much as someone he grew up with, someone he'd planned a life with. A woman who'd waited for him to come home, tied ribbons around oak trees for him.

A woman who'd loved him as much as I do.

"Because when Allison died, I gave up. I was so angry. I hated people... God, country, everything that had stolen the time we should've had together. The family we might've had. The family I thought I'd never have."

Tears are in my eyes. I love this man, and even as he's telling me about the broken dreams he had with another lover, it twists pain in my chest to think he felt such loss. "Oh, Derek. I'm so sorry."

To my surprise, though, his voice is optimistic. "Stop." He catches me around the waist, pulling me onto his lap. His hands are at my neck, and his thumbs sweep the tears from my cheeks almost as fast as his lips smooth them. "Please don't cry. I know... what happened was unfair. I spent so many years bitter about it."

Nothing seems right to say, so I only nod, looking down.

"Melissa, listen to me. You were... you are something I thought I'd never have. And our baby..." He pulls me closer, and he's holding my neck with his head resting above my heart. "You helped me forgive the past and find peace. I love you so much. Why do you think I'm so hell bent on protecting you?"

I understand what he's saying. It's beautiful, and it mirrors the hope he gave me that short week in the desert. "I can't bear thinking of how you suffered, losing her like that."

"During that time we were apart—the time before you came to me with what Sloan had done, when I was only waiting, hoping you felt the same—I realized love isn't something you can give away or shut off when it doesn't work out. When love is taken away, it creates a vacuum that has to be filled with new love. You were a gift I wasn't looking for, a gift I didn't deserve, and maybe that's why you're so precious to me. You're my second chance... and you gave me a second chance. Twice."

My arms are hugged between us, and I slide my hands up to hold his face. "You've never told me this before."

"I don't want you to be threatened by my past." He turns his head to kiss my palm. "You're strong and beautiful, and it's what I love about you. I can't wait to see what our future will be."

His words wash away my fears in a flood of understanding. He said exactly what I needed to know. Our love isn't a competition. There are no ghosts lurking in the background, only memories. Some are good, some bad, but we're something new. We're building our future together, and in my heart, I know it's right, because as much as I love him, I would never want him to go through life alone, and I know anyone who felt the way I do about him would say the same.

"I want to go to Baltimore with you." I don't have to think about it. "We shouldn't be apart anymore."

"No. I want you to stay here. Elaine can stay with you and—"

"Sloan doesn't scare me. He doesn't own me, and he can't win—"

"Anything with the power to take you away from me scares me."

I'm shocked by his answer. Derek isn't supposed to be afraid of anything. "Nothing is taking me away from you."

He catches both my hands in his. "I won't risk you or the baby being hurt. We'll end the long distance arrangement after we finish this job."

"How long?" After all he just said to me, I feel our pending separation more acutely than ever.

"A week? Two tops, and I'll keep in touch with you the entire time."

"Two weeks? That's longer than we've spent apart since Christmas."

"Believe me. I'll be doing everything in my power to make it end sooner." His phone buzzes, and when he looks at the face, he starts to rise. "It's Patrick. We've got to get moving."

Tears heat my eyes as I follow him back toward my house. I'm not sure I'll be able to hold it together until he's away. "It hurts more than ever this time." My voice is soft, and I'm fighting as hard as I can. It's difficult between my fears for him and what he just shared — and a healthy dose of pregnancy hormones. Still, I don't want his last sight of me to be crying.

I follow him back to my bedroom, where he stops and hugs me close. My face is against his chest, and his fingers thread into my hair at the base of my neck. Several seconds pass and we only hold each other, sharing our breath, melting together. Another buzz from his damn phone, and he releases me.

Quickly he pushes his clothes into his duffel and takes the keys. In the kitchen he stops and pulls me close again. "I promise not to prolong this." Turning me to the side, he puts a large hand over my tiny baby bump. "Love you," he whispers, and I catch his cheek, guiding his lips to mine.

I'm off the floor in his embrace. Mouths open, tongues unite, I'm kissing him like he's headed into battle, which in a sense he is. My only comfort is Patrick's promise to have his back.

Another buzz, and I almost forget I'm on Team Patrick now. "I don't want you to go." I whimper.

"I know." He sets me down and gives me a peck on the nose, another on the forehead as he inhales deeply. "I love your scent."

"I love you."

"Love you more."

And with that, he's gone.

CHAPTER 9: NOT THE GOOD GUYS
DEREK

Baltimore is cold and windy when we arrive. Patrick's booked us three rooms in the Four Seasons on Harbor East—perfect for our setup, and close to potential hook-up locations. I've promised Melissa to make this happen as quickly as possible, but the truth is, we've got to establish ourselves in this location, make a plan, and scout the best place for the ultimate encounter.

Toni arrived the night before, and she's asked to go by Star Brandon again for this gig. Seems that's her go-to alias. We meet at the bar for our first planning session.

"You don't think Star sounds too... hooker-ish?" Patrick is frowning as he studies the drink menu.

Toni... or Star is wearing a cream, Calvin Klein dress that hugs her slim body and ends mid-thigh. Her long hair is now wavy and colored light brown, and she's wearing about eighty percent less makeup than at the Skinniflute. Light-brown eyeliner and mascara, pale pink lips. I hate to admit it, but she does resemble Melissa. She's hot.

"You fell for it." Her mouth is the only thing that gives her away—and her husky smoker's voice.

"You were also a blonde." Patrick laughs and has the decency to appear ashamed of himself.

I lift the tumbler of Scotch I ordered. "You're going to have to fix your delivery to catch Sloan's interest."

Instantly, her voice turns soft and high, slightly breathy. "My delivery? Is this what you mean?" She blinks up at me with doe eyes.

"Shit," I sip the beverage. "I don't get to say this very often, but Patrick was right. You're good."

She smiles and lifts the vodka she ordered, holding it out to clink my glass. "Trust me, big boy. I'll nail this bastard for you."

"That's the only reason I'm here." I give her tumbler a bump.

Patrick lifts his drink off the bar and takes her elbow. "Let's find a place where we won't be overheard."

In a corner booth near the back of the hotel bar, we group close together to strategize. "Bennett is keeping tabs on Sloan, putting together a schedule of his week, his favorite haunts."

"Why am I here?" Star's watching me. "I mean, what reason do I give for being in the city?"

Fuck, she's smart. "I can tell you've done this before. What are you comfortable doing? What's familiar?"

"Patrick fell for me being a temp. I could say I'm with Contemporary Staffing?"

My partner leans back to sip his drink. "Is that classy enough for our guy?"

Thinking about what I know, I study the table. "It's probably the best thing. It's why you need extra money. Perhaps you've come up from DC?"

"Where I was shagging a senator." Her dark eyes twinkle, and I'm mildly disturbed that her alibi is so believable.

"Yes. It'll appeal to his ego. You're good enough for the powerful."

Patrick nods. "Now we just need to work out the initial encounter and hooking him."

"I'll hook him." Star's eyes slide over to my partner. "I give a hell of a hummer, remember?"

Clearing his throat, Patrick stands. "I need a fresh drink. Anybody else?"

I nod. "Thanks." When he's away, I turn back to Star. "You'll probably have to meet him more than once to get us what we need. I doubt he gets rough the first time. How do you feel about that?"

"I want to work out with you guys."

That wasn't the answer I expected. "What does that have to do with—"

"Yes." She's dead serious, so I hold back and listen. "I'll probably have to fuck him at least once before we get what we need, but I've been taking kickboxing classes. I want you guys to help me get stronger."

My eyes narrow. "What's on your mind?"

She doesn't miss a beat. "Revenge."

The workout room at the Four Seasons is state of the art, as to be expected in a five-star hotel, but I catch a cab to the Druid Hill YMCA instead. Patrick takes the city bus; Star takes the Metro. We don't want to be seen together too much around our location.

Bennett has verified we can stage an encounter with Sloan easily in Little Italy. It seems our target is a

Thursday night regular at the Oceanaire Seafood Room. It's perfect, and gives us a few days to scout more secluded spots nearby. Somewhere Star can take him where Patrick and I can be in the shadows, waiting.

"I can't wear a wire." Star is curling the bar I've loaded for her with fifty pounds. "If he starts exploring under my clothes, it's too risky."

We're in a somewhat private area of the gym, but we still need to be speaking in code. "The last thing I'm interested in is hearing you interact with him, but you're all we've got in terms of capture."

Patrick's nearby curling dumbbells. "It's true, and I don't like you getting too far out of our reach with him."

Star curls one more time and puts the bar down. "So you two get a peep show." She shrugs. "I've done worse for an audience."

My partner puts down the weights and picks up his towel, holding it in front of his mouth as if he's wiping away sweat. "What are you planning? I expect it'll take two… maybe three encounters before he'll show his true colors. Hopefully, not more."

"First night, drinks, making out, BJ most likely." She's holding her towel in a similar fashion as Patrick, over her face, pressing it to her forehead. I'm sitting on the bench, leaned forward doing curls, pretending not to listen as she continues. "Second night, more of the same, penetration. Third night, kick his ass."

Sick fills my stomach. All of this is messed up, and it's the only way we're taking my fiancée's stalker off the grid. His lawyers will have a hard time arguing against a battered hooker full of Sloan's DNA. I can't wait to see them try.

"You sure you're okay with this?" Regardless of her past experience or what she claims, I can't help asking one more time.

Her expression is hard and flat when she answers me. "Yes. I'm helping you, but I'm also doing this for Tiffany. Now let's hit the bags."

Kickboxing.

That evening at the hotel, I'm dead. Strength training is one thing, but strength training combined with two hours of kickboxing is over my limit. My phone has a few missed texts from Melissa, but instead of texting her back, I call.

The sound of her eases the tension in my chest. "Where have you been all day?"

"At the Y. Strength training and kickboxing."

"Kickboxing?" Her voice goes high. "Honey, I wasn't implying anything yesterday morning…"

That makes me laugh, remembering our conversation in bed. "We're helping our bait get better prepared to defend herself."

"You sound tense again." Her playful tone is gone. Worry and guilt are in her voice, and my arms long to hold her. "I hate this so much. I hate remembering he's out there, thinking of that poor girl facing him alone. For me."

"Star is *not* a poor girl, trust me."

"Star?"

Lying back on the bed, I rub my forehead. "That seems to be her stage name, so we're going with it."

"I guess if she's taking the risk, she gets to call a few shots."

"I don't like it any more than you do." Sitting up, I study my hand, clenching it into a fist and relaxing. "I've gone over it so many times in my mind, trying to find another way."

She exhales. "What if you're wrong and I'm not in danger?"

"I'm not wrong, and I won't let him even think about coming near you."

"Okay, but just for a moment… what if he's moved past me?"

Everything in my experience knows that's not true. Melissa belongs to Sloan in his eyes, and he'll be back for her. But I know it's important for her to feel like she's not the only reason we're here.

So I give her something else to think about. "You said it yourself—there's always another Jessica Black. He's got to be taken off the streets."

She doesn't answer, and for a few moments, we're quiet. "How much longer will you be away?"

"Thursday night will be our first contact. We expect it'll take a few meetings before he relaxes enough to get rough." I look out at the setting sun, thinking of all the people living normal lives, doing regular things right now. One day soon, that will be me again. "I expect it to be like I said, two weeks tops."

"I miss you." Her voice is sad, and I want to lighten the mood.

"What did you do today?"

Sounds of her moving through her house fill my ear. I can almost see her walking, her dark waves swaying down her back. "Had lunch with Mom, finished Bea's online storefront. If I were there, I could meet with her in person and be with you."

I shake my head, even though she can't see me. "It's too risky, and if you're seen here, it could put him on alert. It could jeopardize the whole plan. Just hang tight, okay?"

"Elaine and I'll probably trade off spending the night together."

"That's a great idea. You can keep each other company."

"She'll be sexting with Patrick the whole time."

My eyebrows rise. "I'll keep you company then."

"I'd rather do it in person. I could be waiting for you when you get in. Massage that stress away… kiss your skin… naked." Her words register right below my belt, causing me to shift in my seat.

"Forget the sexting, let's talk it out now. What are you wearing?"

"Maternity clothes at last!"

I laugh. "How's the baby?"

"It seems like I'm showing even more since yesterday." Sadness gone, I can hear her excitement rising. "I really want us together when he starts moving."

Closing my eyes, I can see her gorgeous body, full breasts, stomach just starting to round out. "When can we find out if you're right?"

"Twenty weeks is when they usually do ultrasounds for gender."

It's getting close. "I'll be there. Take care of you both."

The warmth is back. "Love you."

"Love you more."

We say goodnight, and for a moment I lie on the bed thinking. If there were any way she could be here, damn straight I'd have her here yesterday. In the meantime, I'll hit the shower. We're on our own for dinner, and since my partner is apparently occupied, I want to check out a local jewelry store for something platinum and diamond encrusted.

Thursday couldn't arrive soon enough, but now that we're on the verge, our plan feels shakier than ever. We spent the day yesterday locating a private spot off an alleyway. A closed balcony that's above and somewhat hidden is attached to the restaurant. Patrick managed to talk the staff into letting us use it, and from what he says, he didn't have to give any information away.

He and I will be up there monitoring, where we can drop down if needed. Star will lead Sloan into the dark alley and do whatever she needs to do. Once the ball is rolling, we'll tune out unless she gives us the signal.

The real action shouldn't occur before next week. I'm actually hoping it will, but I have nothing to base it on besides my gut. The true timeline could be longer or shorter.

While we'd waited for Patrick to work his magic on the restaurant staff, Star and I had checked out the access in and out of the small lane that runs behind the businesses.

It seems to have been intended for deliveries, but most the doors are welded shut or appear unused. She watches as I try them, one after the other.

"You don't approve of me." She's following me a few steps behind, and today she's in black leggings and boots, topped off by a short bomber jacket and white sweater that doesn't even cover her ass.

"You came into my office, set up my partner..." I grunt as I push on another sealed door. "No. It's safe to say I *don't* consider you one of the good guys."

She pulls her long, brown hair over her shoulder in an elegant sweep. Again, I'm impressed at her ability to shrug off the white trash so easily. "I'm sorry I fucked with Patrick, but I didn't have the whole story. And I needed the money."

"You fucked with my business, my reputation. It's the same as if you fucked me."

"I think I'd remember that." Her voice is soft, and she smiles up at me.

I shake my head. I'm not sure if she's attempting to mend bridges or flirt, but I'm not interested in either option. "You'll need to be here for us to see you." Pointing to the black metal door with the orange band across the bottom. "Can you remember this door? It's pretty distinctive."

"I think I'll remember it."

"Okay." I nod and head back up the alley to where Patrick's supposed to meet us. This should work.

Once we're together at the top, she tries again. "I've never seen a man like you do that before."

My brow lines. "What are you talking about?"

"That day in Raleigh, when you left so fast and took Patrick's car." Her arms are crossed and she looks genuinely concerned. "It's hard to believe someone like you can feel fear."

"Everyone feels fear." I look at my hands again. "Just target the one thing they can't live without."

I close my fist, and I can't help thinking I could end this, no charade necessary.

She touches my arm. "I decided that day I'd do whatever you asked. What do you want me to do?"

For a second, I'm confused. Then I realize she's talking about Sloan. "Oh. I don't know." I exhale deeply. "I'm not looking to be judge, jury, and executioner here. I just want whatever it takes to put him away for good."

"If you're not judge, jury, and executioner, then you don't want him out of your life permanently." Her dark eyes hold mine, and I can see she's waiting for me to say the word. It's hard to believe this small woman might be capable of doing anything more forceful than turning state's witness.

"You're wrong. I do want him out of our lives permanently."

She's still holding my gaze when I hear Patrick approaching.

"Okay!" His breezy voice breaks through the tension. "I've got it all set up. Derek and I'll be on the balcony. It's closed, so you won't hear us, but we'll be there... What's going on?"

He stops in front of us, and I know my partner's too smart to be fooled. "What's the plan if Star gets in over her head?"

"I won't." Her voice is sharp and argumentative. "You two just stay back and let me handle it. Don't fuck up our case being overprotective."

Patrick nods. "Safe word. You need a safe word, T."

"What the hell?" She's confused, but I see where he's going with it. He's right.

"What's something you can yell that you'd never say during sex?"

A laugh bursts from her mouth with an exhale. "Sangria?"

"Can you yell that?" Patrick's running it over in his mind, and I can tell he approves already. "It's good because it won't alert the other patrons. They'll think it's just some drunken diner..."

"Hell, it won't even alert him if he's not paying attention." I'm irritated that Star's smart. She could do more with her life than this.

"Sangria it is." Patrick leads us out of the alley. "Now we just have to get changed, head to the bar and wait."

Hours later, we're back at the Oceanaire.

Patrick is the only one in the bar with Star. He's not even with her; he's down a few seats nursing a vodka tonic. Sloan knows me, so once they're situated, I head to the secluded balcony to wait.

The staff doesn't even look up when I pass through the side hall off the kitchen and dash up the narrow flight of stairs.

I've only seen this spot from the outside. Inside is a whole different story. It's technically not a balcony. It's more like a closet with a window that opens. It's tight and cramped, and it smells like musty socks and body odor. I cover my nose with my hand, thinking this is going to be a long night. What I'm pretty sure is a used condom lies discarded in the corner.

Apparently this is a hot spot for hookups. My first thought is we should've put Star here, but then she would've been too inaccessible. My second thought is what the hell did Patrick say he and I would be doing up here? Fuck it. I can't worry about that now.

I text him to turn on the surveillance app, so I can hear what he's seeing. His phone will be out on the bar, and the technology's not perfected. I'll get plenty of noise along with the conversation through my earbuds, but I'll be able to follow what they're saying.

He texts back they're not in place yet, and I have to wait. Tension tightens the muscles in my abdomen. Fucking surveillance. I've never liked how much waiting was involved in this part of this job. It's a big reason private investigative work lost out over corporate when Stuart and I set up the firm. I feel around the one small window looking for a latch to release it. If we have to get down there fast, one of us can jump. Pushing it open and looking down, I decide that'll be Patrick's job.

A blip on my phone, and I know the subject's in the building. I'm so tense, the muscles across my upper back ache. Star's competent. She's demonstrated her street smarts and experience. She's committed to this job for more reasons than just helping us. But right now is our most important moment. If this blows up, we could lose our licenses. We could be arrested for entrapment...

This has to work.

I slip the earbuds in my ears. Noise.

The ting of ice against crystal, crash of liquor bottles against racks.

Voices are speaking, but I don't hear anything familiar.

Finally, a voice I do recognize cuts through the din.

"I'm sorry." Star's tone is breathy and high. Marilyn Monroe. "Do you mind if I wait here? I'm supposed to be meeting someone."

"Of course not." Sloan is casual, but I'm a guy. There's a spark of interest there.

Tonight, she's wearing a filmy black dress that ends at her knees. It's got a high slit on the side and thin straps over her shoulders, so it's clear she takes care of her body. We got her a very light golden spray-tan and her hair is styled loose down her back. A silver cuff bracelet, thin necklace, and small hoop earrings are her only accessories. She's classy, but also sexy enough to get the wheels turning.

The noise of the bar is loud in my ears, and I can only imagine what's happening. Bartenders moving fast, patrons waiting to put in drink orders. Finally, Sloan orders a Manhattan. Star already has a cosmopolitan—a drink she says is for wannabe little bitches. Whatever. So long as she keeps all that to herself.

"Oh," more Marilyn. "I'm sorry again. It's so crowded here tonight. Is it always like this?"

"Thursdays are the busiest night here." Sloan sounds relaxed—I'm not sure if that's good or bad. "They get the local crowd combined with the tourists just arriving."

She breathes a soft laugh. "I wonder which of those I'd be."

"You're not from Baltimore?"

"No, I'm a tourist hoping to become a local."

"So you're relocating."

It's pretty banal stuff, but at least she's got him talking.

"I hope to. I'm supposed to be meeting someone from Contemporary Staffing, but it looks like they're not coming."

They're quiet for a few minutes. Did she lose him? Fuck. If he walks away, we're left with nothing. A desperate hooker is way too suspicious for his taste.

Another agonizing minute passes.

At last a voice, but it's not either of the ones I want to hear. "Your table's ready Mr. Reynolds."

Shit.

"Well, good luck to you, Miss…"

"Brandon. Star Brandon."

"Sloan Reynolds. Nice chatting with you."

It's quiet again, and my gut sinks. Now what?

Just as I was pulling out the earbud his voice comes back. "If you're still here in a little while, I'll be back at the bar after dinner."

Star's voice is a sexy purr. "I won't go anywhere."

Now it's back to waiting. And hoping he doesn't have second thoughts and order dessert.

CHAPTER 10: ALL I SEE
MELISSA

Channel after channel passes on the screen, but nothing interests me. I can't help wondering what might be happening miles away in Baltimore, and I chew my lip as I watch the talking heads blink and disappear, one after the other. I'm about to give up and start Internet shopping when my phone buzzes.

Snatching it up, I touch my best friend's picture on the face. "Hey, what's up?"

Elaine's voice is pouty. "Are you as frustrated as I am?"

I fall back on the sofa. "Not yet, but I'm used to the weekly drought. Check with me tomorrow. I'll be climbing the walls I'm sure."

"After being with Brian you'd think I'd be used to it. Hell, I think my hymen grew back when we were dating."

That makes me laugh. "You're so crazy. That doesn't happen."

"Now I'm completely screwed." She crunches something in my ear. "I've gotten used to Patrick being in my panties every night—I don't know what to do when he's gone."

"Haven't you been doing it over the phone?"

"Mmm…" Another crunch. "That's actually *more* frustrating. He tells me all this dirty stuff he wants to do to me, and he's a million miles away! It's awful!"

"You're supposed to finish while you're on the phone, dum-dum."

"I'm still all achy and needing him." I hear her sit up fast. "Do you have a dildo?"

Laughter bursts out of me then. "I have Derek."

"Not all week! What are you hiding? I bet you have a stash."

Picking up the remote, I start the kaleidoscope of channels again. "I hate to disappoint you, Miss Gold Tie, but I'm not hiding a toy collection."

"Hmm. Neither am I. We should do some research tomorrow night when I'm there."

"What are you eating?" I'm back to watching the faces flash past on the screen.

"Popcorn. Do you want me to run by the store before I come over? After school?"

"Yes. Get chips and salsa, guacamole, tamales…"

"Real and virgin margaritas." She pauses for a moment. "Are you doing okay? Really? This has to be bothering you."

I stop switching channels on a talent competition and hit mute. "I'm not sure how I feel. Derek's so convinced I'm in danger, and I can't change his mind. I won't let my mind travel to what he might do—the lengths he might go to."

"Patrick's there. He won't let anything happen they can't sit on. Or get out of."

I know she's right, but I know something more. My mind drifts to my conversation with Patrick a week ago. "He promised me…"

Elaine keeps talking. "I gotta be honest, I don't know how you two can keep up the long distance. I *hate* it."

"No shit. I'm starting to remember how obnoxious you were before Patrick relocated." Bending my elbow so I can prop my head on my hand, I gaze out the window at the swaying sea oats. "We've agreed to end it after this job, but even if that means more time for me in Princeton, I'm not giving up my place here."

"I love your cottage. I wish it were warm enough to sunbathe all weekend. You've got the best spot for going topless."

Lying back, I stretch my arms over my head. "One more month and you can attempt to get arrested on my beach all you like."

She laughs. "I have a feeling your beach sees plenty of risky business without me. Besides, we've got connections. See you tomorrow."

"Night, Lainey."

For a few minutes after disconnecting, I lie there and flip through photos of Derek on my phone until I can't decide if it makes me feel better or worse. I stand and go to the kitchen to heat water in the kettle. Maybe chamomile tea will help me relax.

Turning my back to the counter to wait for the whistle, I type up a text. He's probably not in a position to reply, but I want him to know…

Miss you so much. It's hard to sleep outside your arms.

Holding my phone, I think of his lovely face on my pillow. At least the bed still smells like him, even if I'm not clutched tight against his chest. My phone vibrates.

Miss you too. Hope to finish here soon.

Imagining our reunion provokes a little tingle. *I have a special red nightie waiting for you.*

You're beautiful in red.

You're beautiful in everything.

You're beautiful in nothing. My favorite.

A pouty sigh escapes my lips, and I'm as frustrated as Elaine. I want him here now. *Please be careful. Remember Dex and I need you.*

No matter where I am, you are all I see.

My insides melt, and I kiss my phone face before typing. *I love you.*

Love you more. Sleep. I'll be there soon.

I'll try. xxx

With a deep breath, I look once more at the images on my phone trying not to feel miserable. My thumb pauses on a shot of me Derek took a while back. I'm smiling, and my hair's blowing across my face from the side. The little gold heart at the base of my throat catches the light.

Placing my phone on the counter, I snatch up the flashlight and run out to the side porch. Shining it all around, I get down on my hands and knees and feel under the small sofa one more time. Again, I come back with nothing.

Frustrated, I sit back on my heels and look out at the dark night toward the shoreline. The doors are all locked, and I promised Derek I wouldn't do any more night walks until he's back. Still, I can't help wondering if I lost it out there somewhere. Maybe a metal detector…

Just then the whistle starts loud from the kitchen. I push up from the floor, and walk slowly in the direction of the noise as my thoughts travel across the miles to where he is. He's taking a huge risk. Everything could go wrong, and he could lose his license, his business...

Exhaling a tiny prayer to Saint Michael, I take the kettle off the fire and pour the water into my waiting mug.

CHAPTER 11: OPENING ACT
DEREK

Time feels like it stretches on for hours as we wait, wondering if our target will come back or move on. I want to call Mel, but I also want the kitchen staff to forget I'm here. So I keep quiet. Until she texts me.

All the reasons I'm here come rushing back in just a few lines — to protect her, to keep her safe. We say goodnight, and just like that, everything starts to move.

Patrick shoots me a text. *Switch on. We're back in business.*

I quickly put the earbuds back in just in time to hear Sloan talking to Star. Two more martinis, and she's making progress.

"I only waited to tell you goodnight." Her disguised voice is suggestive but tentative. "My rep never showed up, so I guess I'll head back to my hotel now. Alone."

A few seconds pass, and he doesn't respond. I'm hanging on the sounds of glasses clinking and the low roar of voices. He finally speaks.

"How long are you in town?" I'm not sure, but it sounds like a nibble.

"Just a few days." She releases a sad sigh. "I'll head back to DC and look for a new job there, I guess."

"What were you doing before you left?"

"I was an intern for Senator Daltry."

Silence, more noise from the bar. Muffled talking. I can't tell if that was them or what happened. Then they're back.

"...wouldn't mind a little company." I missed the first of that, but it sounds promising. "We can discuss it tomorrow night if you'd like to have dinner with me?"

"Oh, I'd love to!" The gushy sound of her voice worries me. She doesn't need to be too easy. "I really want to stay in the city."

The noise is muffled again, and then the voices vanish altogether. I'm straining against the tiny white headphones. *What's going on?*

Footsteps outside the door, and it pushes open. Patrick shoves inside, and I realize he put his phone in his coat and headed up here.

"She did it." He hangs by the window, scanning the alley. "This is good. One of us can get down there fast if anything goes wrong."

"I'll let you take that route. I'll use the stairs and the kitchen exit."

He chuckles. "Thanks."

"So what'd I miss? You apparently shoved your phone in your pocket at a critical point."

Pulling it out again, Patrick checks the face. "Our man offered her a job 'keeping him company' while she's in town. Strictly a test-run, of course."

"I heard they're having dinner tomorrow night?"

"Gives us one more day to prepare."

The next day we hit the gym again, but not too hard. Star doesn't want to be tired, but we all feel better knowing we've polished her self-defense moves.

"The first night will probably just be hummers and fingering." Her tone is as casual as if she's tending bar. "Probably don't need to worry too much about martial arts."

"I like knowing you're more prepared." Wiping my face with the towel, I grab a bottle of water.

Her attention turns to Patrick finishing up a set of curls. "What made you take off last night?"

He exhales loudly and drops the weight, going to lean against the wall. We're alone in the small room, so we're being less guarded with our speech. "Did it seem like he was on guard to you? Like he kept looking around?"

She frowns. "Not really. He seemed pretty relaxed, actually, but I guess he does this all the time."

I can tell Patrick's not satisfied, and I know my partner pretty well.

"What did you see?" I move closer and lower my voice.

Patrick shrugs. "It was probably me being paranoid, then. I don't do this all the time."

"Still, what was it?"

"A few times it seemed like he was looking my way. Like he had his eye on me."

Star has joined us in the huddle. "I don't think he's bisexual."

"That's not what I mean. More like he was... curious or something."

"It didn't stop him from propositioning me."

135

Pressing my lips together, I think about what Patrick is saying. "Sounds like tomorrow night you should be somewhere else. Is there another place you can observe and not be seen?"

"I'll go over early and try to find a spot." He turns to Star. "You'll be in the exact same place?"

"That's the plan."

Nodding, Patrick starts to go. "I'm headed back. Don't worry if you don't see me tonight. I'll be there."

I know he will. It's almost three, and we all go our separate ways to reconvene at eight.

Five hours later I'm back in the cramped closet, waiting blind. It's the worst kind of surveillance, even though I know Patrick's out there being our eyes. I'm in the dark space wondering how long before I lose it.

I check my watch. It's eight-thirty now. Pulling out my phone, I read back over the texts Mel and I sent back and forth today. Elaine's spending the night, they're having a Mexican fiesta, a few suggestive exchanges involving red thongs and sheer nighties. I smile.

I'd give anything to be there with her tonight, my unpleasant task behind us. But this problem won't take care of itself, and I'm here to see it through to the end.

More time passes. I lean my head back against the wall and try to rest. There's no fucking way I'm sleeping, but I'm not much for playing with apps, and looking at photos of Mel only gets me more keyed up.

Another thirty minutes pass. I think about what's to come, and what we've got to get through to pin this on Sloan. Then I think about him behind bars and what Star said about wanting him out of our lives for good. We could do all this, and he could still get out on parole. Then what?

My eyes squeeze shut. Now isn't the time to worry about that. It only distracts me from our plan, from what we have to make happen here.

Checking my watch, I'm sure they've had dinner at this point. It's after nine, and it's getting nice and dark in the alley. Just then the door pushes open and my adrenaline kicks up a notch.

"Show's starting." Patrick pauses to catch his breath. "Crack the window. We should be able to see them."

I move to the small window and give it a push. Straining into the night, I locate the black door with the orange stripe across the bottom. It's almost directly below us.

"That's the spot. She knows where to go."

We hang out a few minutes, and I'm about ready to ask if he came up too soon when we hear shuffling outside below us. A scuff of heels followed by the slamming of a door.

The acoustics are bad, and the sound echoes up to where we are louder than I expected—or wanted. The click of heels on pavement is clear as a bell, and shortly after, we're bathed in a soundtrack of female moans and gasps. *Shit.*

"This is great," I grumble, but Patrick shoves his elbow in my torso.

He communicates in gestures. "If we can hear them, they might hear us."

Shaking my head, I turn away from the window, but listening is going to be unavoidable, it seems.

Pulling out my phone, I stare at the face again. Patrick stays by the window watching.

Just kissing. He texts.

I'm not really interested in the play-by-play, but I suppose we do need to keep tabs on whether the events are consensual or not.

More gasping punctuated by little moans. "Touch me," Star whispers in an urgent tone. "Touch me."

So far it sounds about as consensual as this setup was intended to be.

A loud moan.

Fingering. My partner texts again.

Great. Just fucking great. My eyes roam up to the ceiling, and I try to think of a million other things.

"Oh, god, yes!" Star's voice breaks the silence. "Oh, god! Don't stop!"

Looking at my hand, I think about how much easier it would be if I just beat him to death.

"Don't stop... oh please... pleeease..." Her voice is high. I'm going to need a workout after this. "Ohh..."

Cries of what I can only assume are an orgasm continue to fill the small space where we're hiding. I can't tell if it's real or fake, and I deny the tightness across my fly. Even Patrick drops his gaze to his shoes, but what comes next snaps us both back to attention.

"On your knees." Sloan's voice is sharp as he gives the order. It's the sound we've been waiting for. "My turn."

"But... I..." She pretends to be confused. Patrick and I both frown at each other... *Is she taunting him so soon?*

Sloan's undeterred. "You came all over my hand, now I intend to fuck your mouth."

The tone in his voice sparks a burn of rage in my stomach. He starts that shit on the first night, it seems. I'm ready to go down and kick his ass, but I feel Patrick's hand grip my arm. His thumb is moving over his phone.

Mine lights up. *She's prepared for this. Let her lay the groundwork.*

Adrenaline is spiking my heartbeat. All I can think of is Melissa being subjected to this fucker's shit, but I hold it together. Shuffling noises meet our ears, and I step forward to see what's happening.

The asshole has his back to the brick wall, and he leans back as Star's head bobs up and down at his crotch. *Shit*. She's going at it.

Stepping back to the wall again, I rub my neck and revisit the plan. It's only the first night. We prepared for this to happen. As many times as I remind myself, this is what she signed on for, I still don't feel any better about it.

Low groans fill the air now. A male hiss, and I'm glad I haven't eaten. Patrick's still watching the whole thing, his hand held out in a "Wait" motion.

Muffled sounds come from Star. A popping noise, and she gasps, laughs a little.

"Good girl," Sloan murmurs to her. "Now all the way... All the way."

More muffled hums. It's quiet a few moments then loud gagging. Patrick straightens up like he's ready to go through the window, and I touch his arm. His thumb flies over his phone face.

Holding her in a deep throat. Can't tell if she's okay.

Coughing, she gasps and laughs again. It's shaky, but *fuck*. I don't know what to do.

"Good?" His tone is condescending, like a coach or a teacher. I want to bash his head against the wall.

"You're so big." Her voice is shaky, but I hear her smile. I rub my forehead, wishing to be anywhere but here.

"Almost there..." His voice is strained and punctuated by the sounds of Star working him. Scuffing of shoes, low groans, then a deep "Ahhh... Drink it all. Fuck yes," which I know is him finishing.

Patrick's lips are tight when I glance up at him.

Star's back to high, breathy Marilyn. "Good?"

"Very good. You can really take it, can't you?" The note of ridicule in his voice makes me hate him even more. I didn't think that was possible.

"I guess." Star's doing the best imitation of timid I've heard in a while, and I'm ready to nominate her for an Oscar.

"No guessing, you can. Next time we'll see just how much you can take, and then maybe we'll discuss my apartment downtown. I'm looking for someone new."

"What does that mean?" She actually sounds excited, and my stomach turns.

"It means treats. And tricks."

"Tricks?"

Sloan's clothes are back in order, and Star leans beside him against the wall. Her black dress is smooth, and only her hair is messy from their encounter.

"You'll see." He touches her hair lightly. "I recently lost someone…"

Tenderness is in his voice. I don't believe it for one fucking second, but we all strain forward anyway, hanging on what he might say next.

"Want to tell me about it?"

Her hand slides across his torso, and for a moment, I think she's going to embrace him — then I notice her black-lace thong peeking out from his pants pocket. He seems to remember as well, and it snaps him out of whatever moment he was just having.

Sloan catches her hand with a menacing smile. "I'll hang onto these. You can have them back tomorrow night."

"When we meet for something more?"

"We'll meet at the bar. Or where are you staying?"

"I'm nearby. The umm… Bridgestreet."

I can see him thinking. "We'd better start at the bar. Here, since you came first, you only get half."

"That wasn't the deal." She slants her eyes like he just told a joke. "What will I do with you?"

He hands over a white envelope. "Just so we're clear, I intend to fuck you tomorrow night. In interesting ways."

"Crystal, and I'll expect the full amount." She rolls forward as if to kiss him, but he pushes up and past her, going back toward the restaurant.

"You'll be full. Don't worry." With that he pushes through the door, leaving her alone.

Bastard.

She rolls back against the wall and looks down at her shoes. I can't tell what thoughts are going through her head. Warring in my chest is a tangle of rage and frustration overwhelmed by a strong need for vengeance.

Star looks up at the window, and her face is serious. She gives us a discreet thumbs-up, then turns on her heel, heading out of the alley.

Back at the Four Seasons bar, nobody speaks as we wait for our drinks. Star passes the envelope containing Sloan's money to Patrick, and he puts it in his jacket pocket like a pimp.

My scotch is the first to arrive, and I consider shooting it. Instead, I pick it up and walk to the square table in the back corner where we can talk privately. The other two join me once they've gotten their drinks.

We're quiet until Patrick finally breaks the awkwardness. "Well, that went about as we expected."

I don't know how the fuck he does it, but with those few words, we're all breathing again.

"He's smooth." Star sounds like she's conducting an autopsy. "And attractive. I can see why the girls go for him."

141

"You're fucking kidding me." I can't believe she just said that.

Her eyes cut to mine. "He's also rich and confident, and he knows his way around a clit." She lifts the glass and takes a sip. "I wasn't faking."

"Well, that's helpful for you, I guess." Patrick follows suit, taking a hit from his drink.

She stares into her vodka. "I see why Tiffany would follow him here."

Her words soften me — now she's speaking language I can understand. For a while at first, I was preoccupied trying to find a reason for this guy's continued success with women. Then I just wanted him gone.

I mutter into my drink. "He apparently has a deceptive opening act."

Patrick keeps us moving forward. "You're all set for tomorrow night. Good work. What's your feeling? Are you ready?"

She shakes her head. "Hope so. He's definitely got a side to him. I wasn't going anywhere without finishing the job tonight. I don't know what would've happened if I'd said No."

"Okay, so that's our plan. Tomorrow night you push back. See if he gets rough." This was Patrick's idea from the start, so I let him lead.

"Is it too soon?" As she speaks, her finger circles the rim of her glass.

"Impossible to know. But I was worried about you tonight. He's one cold-hearted prick."

She looks up and smiles at my partner. "With you, it was fun. With him, I confess. I'm scared."

That does it. "If you want out, say it, and it's over. I don't like any of this."

She looks up, and with her sitting here fucking looking so much like Melissa, I'm about to call it regardless of how she feels. "That's not what I'm saying."

"What are you saying?" Patrick's tone is calming. "We can call it off and walk away. Figure out another option."

"Haven't you tried that already? Isn't that the reason you came to me?" Her glance catches my eyes, but I look down.

It's true, but I don't want to say it right now. I've tried legal methods, and Sloan's slipped out of the noose every time.

"That answers my question," she continues. "I'm doing this for Tiffany. I'm not calling it off. I shouldn't have said I was scared. I'm not."

"You were right to say it." My partner reaches across the table and holds her hand. "Sangria. Okay? We'll be right there."

She nods and looks down again. I'm pissed. "You should be in college or trade school. Why the hell are you even in this line of work?"

And just like that, Toni Durango's back. "Fuck you, Mr. Derek Alexander. What the fuck do you know about what I should be doing?"

I shake my head. "Screw it. I'm getting another scotch. Anybody else?"

Patrick nods, but Star's still nursing hers. "Two drinks it is, then."

I walk up to the backlit bar. It's elegant with dark wood counter tops and recessed lighting. The liquor bottles are arranged in groups all the way to the ceiling by color. They're backlit as well, and it's an impressive mosaic. While I wait for our refills, I look at the two of them sitting, leaning forward over the table.

Whatever he says makes her laugh. She touches his arm, but he pulls away, I know, because of Elaine. Still, he has a connection with her that I don't have—one I don't care to have. I linger a bit after the drinks are placed in front of me before heading back. I'll let Patrick mend that bridge a bit longer.

She's right. We're worlds apart, and I don't have the right to come in and ask for her help then start passing judgment on her lifestyle. It just pisses me off. All of it. I fucking fought for this country. I'm supposed to uphold the law. Turning to the bar, I know I can't go down that path—not if I'm going to do what needs to be done here.

When Star seems more settled, I walk back and retake my seat.

"Okay, we decided we'll have to find a better place than an alley for tomorrow night's rendezvous." Patrick takes his drink and stabs the skinny straw in it a few times. "I'll scout the area and see if I can find something close to the Oceanaire that we can get in and out of discreetly. Maybe this Bridgestreet will work."

"Sounds like tomorrow's assignment."

Star stands and ducks her head in our directions. "I'm heading up if you don't need me for anything else."

"You're off the clock." Patrick's still going for casual, business-as-usual, but I can't do it.

"I'm sorry you had to do what you did tonight."

She blinks a few times and nods. "I'm sorry I went off on you."

"Water under the bridge."

Once she's gone, Patrick leans forward, and speaks low. "Now will you get off my case about fucking her at the office? She's a fucking pro."

"I will never get off your case about that, but you're right. And it's a damn shame." I think about subcultures and the world of the street. How people get trapped in a life of alleyways and dark closets. Most of them stay there until they're dead.

Then I remember my question from earlier. "What did you tell the kitchen staff we were doing in that closet?"

Sitting back in the chair he laughs. "I didn't tell them anything. I just asked if my partner and I could use the room."

Fucker. "That's what I thought."

"Hey, you're a hot piece of ass. I'd do you. If I went that way, I mean."

"I hope I don't have to kick your ass one of these days."

"Get some sleep. We've got to work fast tomorrow."

Down from the Oceanaire are two Bridgestreet hotels. Patrick and I choose the closest one to enter, posing as bankers in town planning a conference. While getting the tour of their facilities, we find a smallish meeting space with both an outside door and an adjacent tech room — complete with two-way mirror. It's perfect. Bonus: It's soundproof.

While the hotel's conference director describes their state-of-the-art networking system, Patrick pockets the extra door card to the room. We'll come back after hours and go over the best way to get in and out. We'll also be sure that outside door is left ajar. Security will be another problem, but I'll see if I can hack into their computer systems and get a feel for his rounds.

All of it has to be perfectly choreographed, but we're ready by the time eight rolls around. Patrick slipped a hand-drawn map under Star's door earlier in the day for her to take and go over alone. We'll be in the tech booth waiting when they arrive.

Star calls my cell, which is unexpected, to let us know she's heading out, and I feel the need to say it one more time. "If there were any other way..."

Her soft exhale passes over the line. "Stop. I agreed to help you for my own reasons. Reasons I'm sure you're too noble to understand."

"I'm not so noble. I understand revenge." We're quiet a moment. "Patrick has the lead here, but I don't like putting you in this position."

"Patrick understands me. I fucked him. I messed with his head. I'm not worth you feeling sorry for."

Their history still ticks me off, but with this, I'm ready to forgive. "You're a human being. You're worth my concern, and you shouldn't have to sell your body."

"Don't confuse sex with intimacy, Derek. My body is not my heart. I can separate what I choose to allow happen to me from who I am."

The rationalizations of the hooker. I've heard them before. "If that's what you want to believe, it's not my business."

"Look, let me use my choices for something good. It's a small sacrifice. And by helping get justice, I can find some level of redemption."

I do understand that, even if it turns my stomach. "We'll be there if you get in trouble."

"Sangria."

CHAPTER 12: TOOTHLESS MONSTERS
MELISSA

My feet are in Elaine's lap and she's massaging them while we watch *Pitch Perfect* for the thousandth time.

"I think I can do that cups trick." Speaking of cups, Elaine's on her third margarita, while I've almost finished the entire chips and salsa by myself.

"Don't. You're drunk and you'll just make a mess."

She swats my foot. "I am *not* drunk!" She struggles to get up, but I push down with my legs, pinning her in place. "Let me up!"

"Seriously, can we please just finish the movie? I told you tequila would make you wild."

"All the little kids do it at my school." She's whining now. "I've been wanting to try."

"I don't have any solo cups."

Pouty face. "Fine. But you can't crush my dream. I'll do the cups!"

I grab the remote to rewind the scene we've missed while she was talking, but the movement pinches my stomach. "Oh, shit. Why did you let me eat all those chips? I'll have heartburn."

"I'm not about to get between a pregnant lady and her snack foods." She takes another wobbly sip of margarita. "Besides, you're in that lucky 'eating for two' stage. Live it up!"

"That's a myth. My doctor said I shouldn't gain more than fifteen pounds with this pregnancy."

She leans forward and scoops up some chip particles from the bottom of the bowl. "Have you seen your fiancé? He's a giant. That baby needs food."

"Not sure chips and salsa count as real food."

She flops back, and we're quiet again, watching. She takes another, longer drink, and my eyes cut to her face. She's not smiling. She's been down since she got here, and I know Lainey well enough to tell it's more than just missing Patrick.

"You okay?" I ask as gently as possible.

A few moments go by, and she blurts it. "I did something really bad."

My brow lines in confusion. I can't guess what in the world she might have done, but I can tell it's seriously bothering her. "Do you want to tell me about it?"

She sits up and puts her margarita on the coffee table, then flops her arms at her sides. "Just... don't lecture me. I know it was wrong."

Eyebrows raised, I nod and take her hand. The anticipation is almost too much.

She takes a deep breath and then lets it out. "I stopped taking my birth control pills last month."

My head ducks forward. "What?"

Her grip tightens on my hand. "You heard me."

"Does Patrick know?"

"No. And I know it was wrong. I was having a really hard month, and then Kenny called, and it made me so depressed. I just felt like… I'm going to lose him, Mel." Her voice cracks, and her green eyes are so round when she looks at me. "I panicked."

"Oh, Lainey!" I reach forward to hug her, but she pulls away, shaking her head.

"I know, it was manipulative and all that… and there's more."

Sitting back again, I chew my lip. Now I'm nervous. "Okay?"

Her voice is thickening, and I can tell she's going to cry. "I pulled this stupid stunt, and… nothing happened. *Nothing*! We must've had sex a hundred times last month, and I started today just like clockwork."

I begin to breathe again. "But that's a good thing, right?"

She nods, but she doesn't answer me.

"Hang on." I roll my awkward self so I can put my feet on the floor and then scoot closer to her, wrapping an arm around her shoulders. "What are you thinking right now?"

"That I'm broken?" She puts her head on my shoulder as the tears fall. "What if I can't get pregnant? I really will lose him… then what will I do?"

At that moment, the show's enormous musical performance erupts from the screen. We both jump, and I scramble for the remote to mute it.

My heart is thumping, but I go back to where she is, taking her hand. "I think you should talk to Patrick about it. He might want to wait on another baby, considering what's happening with Kenny—"

"Yes, Kenny. *She* can have his babies." She cries harder, falling into my lap. "He's going to leave me for her."

149

"Oh my god, he is not! For starters, Patrick doesn't love Kenny, he loves *you*. And jeez, Lainey, it was only one month! Come on..."

Sitting up and shaking her head, she wipes her nose with the back of her hand. "I know it's true. I can feel it in my gut. This is just what I get."

"What you get for what?"

"For being jealous? For thinking evil things about Kenny and her baby..." She sniffs. "I actually hoped —"

"Stop. You have *always* been dramatic. Just because you thought something about your fiancé's baby mama doesn't mean you actually meant it."

"I meant it." Her voice is low and her chin drops. "I'm a horrible person, and now I'm getting what I deserve. I'll never have Patrick's baby, and he'll leave me for her. Just wait and see."

"What the hell! Of all the — I am never letting that boy leave town again! And you're cut off. No more margaritas."

She falls back on the cushions to cry. It's possible she's on a jag, so I try for counter-maneuvers.

"In fact, I might text him right now and tell him you've gone nuts, and it only took one week of him being out of town for it to happen."

She flies back up then. "Don't you dare! I don't want him to know what I've done."

"So far you haven't done anything but play pregnancy Russian roulette and talk like a crazy person."

"He's going to leave me for her, Mel. He doesn't know it now, but he's going to take one look at his little baby boy, and it's going to be over for me."

Catching her cheeks, I lift her face. "Look at me. Yes, Patrick is going to fall in love with his son, but he is insanely in love with you. Nothing is going to change that. He's drawn to you. He can't fight it. You're the candle, and he's the moth."

She blinks tears, and I pull her to me, rubbing her back. "Trust me. I can see what you can't, and as much as I know Patrick would love it if you got pregnant, you need to include him in the planning."

"I know," she sniffs, holding my waist. "I want to believe that."

"Then believe it."

We're quiet for a few moments as her sniffles gradually subside. My thoughts drift to the young woman I've only met once. "Why did Kenny call?"

Elaine sits up and grabs a napkin off the table, blotting her cheeks. "She needed him to cosign for her to get a car loan."

I nod, pressing my lips together. "I thought it might be something with the baby."

"No." She folds the napkin and then unfolds it again. "He called the dealer the next day and just bought it for her, said she doesn't need to worry about a car note."

That makes me smile. "He's really sweet to her." My smile quickly vanishes when I see Elaine's chin drop. Her brow crinkles again, and I grab her hand, hoping to derail any more tears. "They're *friends*. It's a good thing, Lainey. What if she were a raging bitch?"

Her lips press together as she studies the napkin. "You're lucky. You don't have anything threatening your relationship with Derek."

As much as I want to argue she doesn't either, I pause and think about it for a few moments. Even though she's drunk and irrational at the moment—or maybe *because* she is—I let my guard down. "I used to be afraid he'd never love me as much as he loved Allison."

Her face jerks up to mine. "What the hell? Whatever would make you think something like that?"

Shrugging, I look at our hands. "She was his first real love. They dated in high school, she waited for him to come back from Iraq. I can tell she was this wonderful, amazing person, and I—"

"Now who's talking crazy? Derek Alexander is the most threatening man I've ever met in my life, and when you're in the room, he completely changes. It's like he's your personal tame lion."

"Still, she had his heart first, and he mourned her for so long."

"Okay, so you said you *used* to be afraid. What changed?"

"Oh! That's why I'm telling you this." For a moment my old fears had tried to creep in again, but I scoot forward. "I finally just told him. I said it out loud to him."

"And?"

"And it was the best thing I've ever done. He opened up and told me things... I don't think he would ever have said to me otherwise. You know how guys are."

"Patrick will talk, but only when he's in the mood."

"Right!" I relax, leaning back on the cushions. "You need to talk to him about how you feel when he's in that mood."

She shakes her head. "I don't know. It just feels different, and you don't have anything else to be afraid of with Derek. No dark secrets."

"I'm afraid of what might happen tonight." Once the words are out, I wish I'd never said them. Elaine's brow creases, and it's clear she hasn't connected the dots on what could happen if things get out of hand in Baltimore.

"What do you mean? You think Derek might do something—"

"Illegal. Something that if he's caught, he'll be taken away from me. You know how protective he is. He's done things... And I'm afraid he'll do them again, and then I'll lose him."

We're quiet, and Elaine's green eyes travel over my shoulder and out the window. Up and away across the miles to where we both know they're waiting. She blinks, and she's back here with me.

"Patrick won't let that happen. I know he won't. Derek's like a brother to him—a brother he *likes*—and he won't let him... get caught."

She didn't say *let him do it*, I mentally note. "That's what I'm counting on."

Quiet again, we hold hands until she pulls me into a hug. "Isn't there a saying about how if you speak your fears, they lose their power?"

A knot is in my throat, and I'm not sure I believe it. Still I go with her. "It sounds familiar."

"Well, we've said it then. Now our fears have to disappear."

I hold onto my friend. She holds onto me, and we settle in to wait, hoping against hope that our fears are now nothing more than toothless monsters.

Chapter 13: To Slaughter a Pig
Derek

Tonight's watch is different from last night's. Unable to find a way to get Patrick from the restaurant to our hideout without being caught, we'd decided he'd be with me from the start, leaving Star alone with Sloan.

We both sit in silence in the tech booth, waiting. Neither of us knows what's happening in the Oceanaire, and we can only hope she manages to lure him here on her own. If anything else happens, we won't know until it's too late.

It's the worst-case scenario.

"When you were in country, did you ever do a night watch?" Patrick is sitting on the floor, his back against the wall. He's got one of his gloves off, and he's rolling a quarter back and forth across his knuckles. "This reminds me of night watch."

"More like being in the advance party." Going ahead of the battalion into a location, no way of knowing what might happen or what surprises might be waiting. "It's a little like that. Minus the IEDs."

My partner exhales and pulls the glove back over his hand. Then he pushes off the floor and steps over to lean beside me against the counter. "You're right. Military deployment is way fucking worse than this. This is plain old detective work, pure and simple."

"Or police work. Waiting around for what's coming."

Glove back off, he starts with the quarter again, back and forth. "Why'd you become a Marine? Other than you were born to play the part?"

"That's pretty much it." I watch the quarter rotate over his knuckles and think about being a kid, waiting on my dad to come home, hearing my mother softly cry herself to sleep at night. "My dad was a Marine. His dad was a Marine—"

"Phew, sounds like a fun group."

"They weren't so bad."

Patrick exhales. Both gloves are off, and he switches the coin to his other hand, continuing the trick. "When Stuart said he was joining the corps, I wasn't a bit surprised. He'd been perfecting that fucking attitude for years."

"Your brother is a great Marine. He had my back more than once." Checking my phone, it's after ten. I don't know how much longer this could take or when to worry if they don't show.

"You'd better keep the gloves on in case we have to move fast." He stops fidgeting, and puts the quarter back in his pocket, nodding as he pulls on the gloves. We can't afford to leave fingerprints.

I'm pretty sure I've asked before, but this wait is mind numbing. "What made you join the Guard?"

"College. I wasn't academic enough for a scholarship, but my parents couldn't afford to send four kids to school. It seemed like the safest alternative."

I chuckle. "And then you got deployed."

"Yep. Thank you, War on Terror."

"I'm sure you were good at it. I've seen your work."

He nods and for a few minutes, we're quiet. Then he shifts and clears his throat.

"Look, I know what we're doing is pretty raw. I'm sorry I couldn't come up with a more elegant plan, but you've got to get some mud on you to slaughter a pig."

I exhale a laugh. "How long have you been saving that line?"

He grins and his shoulders relax. "A few days."

Then I shake my head, serious again. "I couldn't control what took Allison from me. There was nothing I could do." I pause remembering that sick, helpless feeling as she slowly left me forever. I'd never felt that way in my life, and it almost broke me. "I'll be damned if I sit back and let something take Melissa. Especially if I have the power to stop it."

Just then the outside door creaks, and we both jump. Patrick hits the lights, and I instinctively feel my body preparing to fight.

Patrick's the only one armed. He'd insisted, strike that, *demanded* I leave my gun in my room's safe to "avoid temptation." I'd only agreed because he played the Mel card. It's possible he knows me a little too well.

The door creaks again, and in a fumble of hands and staggering steps, Star backs into the room. Sloan's plastered to her mouth, and from this angle, we can see his hands moving up her thighs, dragging the hem of her skirt with them, quickly revealing her thong. *Shit.* This again.

"Here we go," Patrick says in a voice one click above inaudible.

The pair roll against the wall, and the outside door slams shut. The noise breaks their kiss, and Sloan looks up and around, surveying the small, empty conference room. It's dim-lit by small, emergency lighting and the green glow of the Exit sign.

"How did you know about this place?" His voice is thick.

"Passed it on my way to the restaurant tonight." Star's back to breathy-high Marilyn. "I peeked my head in, and when I saw the side door, I thought of you."

He turns back to her with a greedy smile. "Good call." Then he covers her mouth again with his.

His hands return to her ass, and he lifts her against the wall. A memory of me lifting Melissa in a similar way knots my stomach, and I turn my back. We can hear it. I don't have to watch.

Star's voice. "What if I worked for your company? Then I could see you every day. Or every afternoon?"

Glancing over my shoulder, I see Sloan lower and turn her so that her back is against him. "Not a bad idea." He moves her legs apart with his knee, and his hand goes between her thighs in front, pulling up swiftly.

"Oh!" She lets out a shocked noise, but her cheek is pressed to the side so we can see her face. She isn't in pain. In fact, her expression is just the opposite. It's impossible to know when she's acting. I'm fucking listening for *Sangria.*

"You feel that?" Sloan leans into her ear. "That's where I'm going to fuck you. Right in that tight little hole."

She inhales sharply. "I don't do that for clients." Her hips are following his movements, rocking back and forth. "It's too risky."

His hand appears to be moving all over her crotch, and she lets out a little moan. "Your tight little ass loves what I'm doing, and if you want your money, you'll fuck me like I say. How do I know you're on the pill?"

With a shudder, she moves to the side, quickly evading his hand. "Use a condom if you don't believe me. I'm not getting pregnant."

Anger flashes on Sloan's face, and he steps in front of her, pinioning her. Her resistance is good, but it's too soon. We need his physical evidence in her body before he hurts her.

"Don't fuck with me. I'm going bareback, and I'm going where I want."

Rage tightens my throat. The way he's standing, blocking her face, she could easily be Mel facing down this bastard. It takes all the willpower I possess to stay in this small room and not go out there. I have to distract myself from the photos I've seen, the one of Jessica Black, the one of my beautiful bride's battered face.

Patrick's leaning over the counter near the door, and I see his hand twitch. From his tense stance, I can tell he's ready to intervene as well.

"Look, I don't have any lube." Star steps to the side and around so her back is to us again. "I won't ass fuck without lube."

Rage burns cold in Sloan's eyes. He's controlled, but barely, and by the way his lips part over his teeth, I know tonight will definitely be the night.

"I know where to get lube." He grabs her by the neck and spins her back to the wall, slamming her head hard against the plaster.

Star pushes against him, but it's a clumsy effort. Patrick and I both know her skill at self-defense, and I wonder if she was injured just then. He's back on her just as fast, and with a grunt, she pushes away again. Then she rears back and slaps him hard across the face.

The *SMACK!* echoes in the dark space, and my muscles tense up, ready to take action.

But everything stops.

Sloan steps away from her and turns to face our direction. He looks like a freaking psycho killer in the pale green light, and I swear I can see the wheels going as his eyes travel around the dark room.

Hidden in the small tech booth, neither Patrick nor I breathe. This fucker is smart. He wouldn't have gotten away with his tricks so long if he weren't. My stomach muscles tighten. I have no idea what's about to happen.

He speaks into the darkness. "Where are you..." It's a whispered taunt, and he takes a few steps toward us before whispering again. "I know you're there."

What the fuck? How could he possibly know we're here? Maybe he really is crazy. My heart's slamming in my chest, and tension pulls an ache between my shoulder blades. Patrick's tense; the air is crackling.

"You're playing with me, using my weakness..." My brow lines as I listen to his sinister coaxing. "You know I was there. I got to her when you were gone, and I'll do it again. I'll do it every time, any time I wish... She's mine."

Anger blazes low in my stomach, and I hear him. His message is meant for me, whether he's certain of my presence or not. It's a threat he's sending out, and I know the only way to answer it.

I'm ready to answer it.

He waits a few moments longer. Star's got her back to the wall, breathing heavily, watching him. Finally, he shakes his head, looks down, and turns to her. "You're a beautiful woman. Everything I like in one neat package."

A line pierces her forehead, and I can tell she's as confused as we are by this change.

"Thank you?" She tries breathy-Marilyn as she watches him pace back and forth in front of her.

"You remind me of a past lover. One I remember fondly." He smiles, and a creeping dread moves through me. "Would you like something that belonged to her?"

Star blinks rapidly, and I can tell she's on edge as much as we are. Is he talking about Jessica? Can she handle it if he is?

It doesn't matter. I'm just waiting for an opening, any excuse to make my move.

"A gift?" Her voice only wavers slightly. "But we barely—"

"Something *everyone* might find interesting."

Patrick and I exchange a glance.

Sloan's hand goes into his front pocket, and all three of us brace ourselves. The quiet in our small room is broken by the soft scrape of Patrick's gun coming out if its holster. My partner's ready if Sloan pulls out a weapon.

But when we see what has in his pocket, Patrick lowers the gun.

Sloan's "gift" is significant only to me, and for a moment, I stare dumbfounded at the thin gold chain with the tiny heart dangling from his outstretched hand. Melissa's necklace. He was there, and he took it.

His meaning is complete. Message received.

In that moment something in me shifts, and two things happen at once: I lunge for the door, and Patrick throws his body in front of me, blocking it. The two of us are locked in a power struggle that I'm about to win.

"What is it?" Star's Marilyn-voice floats to us, unaware of the battle happening behind the glass.

"It's what I would give you if you hadn't already stolen it." Those words drop a veil of rage over my vision, and I'm about to throw my partner out of the way.

Patrick's legs are braced against the door. "Derek! Don't blow this," he grunts in a whisper. "Don't let him bait you."

I'm so fucking insane with fury, I can barely see, but somehow I mange to find control. I know Patrick's right. We don't have evidence yet, and Sloan's fishing. If he knew for sure we were here, he would've already bolted.

It takes all the willpower I possess to step away from the door. I'm breathing hard, and I pace the small room, waiting. Just waiting. Counting slowly as I step— left, right, left... One, two, three...

Slowly coming down.

"It's a heart." Star takes the necklace from him. "I stole your heart? Are you joking?"

"Are you?" His voice is ridiculing again, and he shoves her back against the wall, his forearm pressing against her collarbone and throat. "Do you think I'm that easy to play?"

Her face begins to turn red, and her eyes squeeze shut. His forearm is right across her esophagus, and a gasping wail comes out. We wait on edge as he rams his hand in her crotch working her hard.

"You think you're going to fuck with me?" His face is leaned close to her ear, and it looks to me like she's fighting tears. "You like that?"

In an instant, Patrick and I are once again locked in a power-struggle for the door.

"Let me go, Patrick, it's too much." My voice is a strained whisper.

I could overpower him, but he stops me. "She can get out of that hold." Patrick hisses back. "Don't blow the job. Just give her a chance."

She snorts louder, and the dim light catches moisture on her upper lip. My chest collapses. I'm not sure she's getting out of this, and I'll be damned if I fucking let him kill her with us steps away.

"*Move*, Patrick." I push against him once more, but his legs are braced. His entire body is levered against mine, and I can tell he's using all the strength he has to keep me in this room.

Sloan's voice cuts through our struggle. "You like that, don't you. Fucking cunt. I have all the power here."

Star's face is turning purple, and I'm about to lift Patrick off the ground when we both hear her mumbling. We stop fighting and wait, looking intently through the two-way glass.

Sloan also pauses, loosening his pressure on her neck. "Are you begging, my love?"

She mumbles again, repeating the word in a whisper. "Sangria..." Her knees buckle, and she crumples to the floor.

Patrick is weightless in my grasp, and I realize he's off the door, spinning toward it. I follow him through faster than Sloan can react.

My partner's headed for Star. Light reflects off the gold chain in her limp hand. I'm headed straight for Sloan.

The last words out of the bastard's mouth are. "What the fuck?"

In one practiced motion, he's in my grasp, both my hands on the sides of his skull. Heat radiates between his skin and mine, and I don't waste a second doing what I know to do, what I'm trained to do.

To end this.

163

To answer his threat and protect her forever.

A swift twist, and a deeply satisfying *SNAP!* travels through the bones of my wrists, up my arms, over my shoulders to my brain. I release him, spreading my hands wide, and Sloan Reynolds drops like a stone, dead at my feet.

My breath is coming in pants, and my arms lower to my sides as I stand over him. The entire room seems to have moved out from me, and I'm alone in a space looking down on what I've done. Waiting to feel something.

Waiting.

Seconds tick by on the clock, and at last it comes.

Satisfaction unrolls like a slow wave in my chest, unfurling like wings through my arms and legs, down my torso to my fingers and toes.

In my peripheral vision, I register Patrick moving swiftly, his voice low. "Fuck fuck *Fuck*. Okay. Well, good riddance. Now we've gotta act. *Fast*."

I step over and gently take Melissa's necklace from Star's weak hand. She's breathing more normally now, despite the tears trickling down her cheeks. Still, she's not weeping. She seems to be recovering, rebuilding her own tough exterior, getting the shield back in place. I'm familiar with that.

Straightening again, I watch as Sloan's body twitches like a dead snake.

Patrick helps Star to her feet and gives her a hug. "Enemy combatant handled," he whispers and pulls off one of his black gloves. Handing it to her, he gives a gentle order, "Take this. Wipe every place you touched him, and get those pants good and down, soldier."

I can't seem to move as they work. It's not out of guilt, because I know with every ounce of certainty I possess I'd fucking do what I just did again and again.

A strong hand grips my shoulder. "Hey. Snap out of it and get the fuck out of here. We're behind you."

Patrick's back to wiping everything with his one glove and Star's slowly doing the same. "*Go!*" He hisses.

With a black-gloved hand, I grasp the outside door and wait, listening. The only sound is the two of them cleaning, punctuated by a quiet sniff every few seconds from Star.

I rub my hand up and down on the doorframe and handle, wiping it clean, but just as I'm about to step through it, a dull thud comes from behind me. It's followed fast by another, and another. *Whop whop...*

Turning back, I see Star kicking Sloan's dead body in the stomach hard. Her voice is cold with anger, and tears stripe her cheeks. "That's for Tiffany, you fuckwad. I hope you're rotting in fucking hell right now." Then she lands a stomping blow to his chest, adding in a low whisper. "That's for me."

She pivots slightly and pulls back to make another blow, but Patrick catches her leg. "Not the head. It might fly off."

Her eyes cut to me, and my brow is creased as I nod. I guess we're more alike than I'd care to admit. I understand her primal need. I know the satisfaction she feels kicking him. She'd probably enjoy punting his head across the room.

Rubbing my eyes, I force these macabre thoughts to stop. I come back out of the rabbit hole, and continue out the door. Patrick's right. We've got to go.

I silently make my way down the hedge-lined alley along the back of the hotel. We have a long stretch of conference-room windows to get past before we're out of range, and I'm hoping Star's recovered enough to walk normally by the time they make it to the end of our leafy covering.

Dark window after dark window, I'm moving fast, thankful it's way after hours. Patrick and I are both trained for stealth, but our injured colleague isn't. I hold up at the edge of the building, where the tall shrub ends and listen.

It seems I've made it, and I yank the black gloves off my hands, shoving them into my pockets. Looking back, Star's leaning on Patrick's arm as he basically carries her down the hidden path. He stops when he reaches me, and leans her against the wall. She watches as he pulls off his gloves and puts them in his pockets.

His voice is low. "We need to act as inconspicuous as possible. The Four Seasons is only a few blocks. Can you make it?"

She nods barely, and it does nothing to ease the adrenaline surging through my veins.

I don't know how to place what I've done, where to put it in my mind or how to wrap my head around it. I've had to kill before, but in this case... What I've done is something outside the law. It's vigilante justice, and it's a cold fact that I'm not sorry.

How can I ever explain this to Mel? What will she think? She says I'm a hero, but I don't know if she can love this side of me. The side that won't back down, that will kill without hesitation.

I can't worry about that now — it has to wait, and we have to move. I step out from behind the hedge, walking straight, hands in pockets. I don't slow or look around.

Bodies pass me, but nobody appears to pay attention to another random person heading to his hotel. No one knows what I've done. I keep going straight. Patrick will wait several minutes before following me out, and we'll rendezvous at the bar and decide what to do next.

Years seem to pass before we've got our drinks and are secreted away at the small back table.

Patrick takes a long hit of vodka before cutting the tension with his usual levity. "I think it's safe to say that did not go as expected." He pauses, studying our shell-shocked expressions. "And shit, I will *never* fucking get used to that sound."

My eyes cut to him, but I can't answer. Breaking bones *is* a sickening sound. Only this time, for me it was a sick satisfaction.

"We're lucky that prick's parents are dead," he continues. "He ran Melissa off, and apparently he killed the only remaining person who loved him. I need another drink." He turns to Star. "You okay?"

She nods, and we're both silent as he leaves us alone again. My eyes are on the amber liquid in my glass, and I feel her eyes on me. No telling what's going through her mind right now. We don't even try to address it. We're both in that place of trying to sort out what just happened, how we feel about it, and what to do with it.

It seems quick when Patrick's back, dropping into his chair, slapping me hard on the shoulder. "You are one strong-assed motherfucker, you know that? At one point, I was sure I couldn't hold you any more. I should've known I wouldn't be able to stop what was coming."

I shake my head and actually laugh. It's kind of a loose laugh, but Patrick is such the fucking little brother I never had.

At last, Star speaks, and she's back to her normal low, smoky contralto. "What happens now?"

Her question snaps me to attention. It's time for me to shake it off. Man up, and be the leader I am. Scooting forward in my chair, I reach for her hand. Our next steps have been circling in my mind since we left the Bridgestreet.

"The best thing would be for you to go to the police. Tell them you were hooking up with some guy you just met, robbers broke in and attacked you both. You ran away scared—don't even mention you know what happened to him."

"If I don't know what happened to him, why would I go to the police?" She's not challenging me, just curious.

"She's right." Patrick leans forward on the table. "I think we should lay low and see what happens. If she thinks he's alive, why would she involve the police? She could get herself in needless trouble, and I wiped everything I could find."

For a moment, I press my lips together and think like a cop. I replay the whole scene in my mind again. "I ran my gloves over all the door handles. Unless he's got her DNA on him somehow."

"He hit me, but he didn't scratch me."

"He had his hands all in your snatch, in your ass…"

She chews her lips, and her eyes drop to her glass.

"That's okay," Patrick cuts in. "He's in a place he shouldn't be with his fucking pants around his ankles and his dick out. Nobody at his company's going to want that publicity. They'll cover that shit up, you watch."

I glance around the small bar, and for now, we're the only ones in it. *Is it possible we could get away with this?* I'm still calming my thoughts, but it seems like we might actually walk.

"The best way for a crime to be discovered is to have more than one witness." My gaze travels from Patrick to Toni, a.k.a., Star. "Patrick and I have done things; we have experience keeping things to ourselves…"

Toni's eyebrows shoot up. "Are you saying you don't trust me?"

I work to even my tone. "There's nothing stopping you from one day using this—"

"Other than the fact I'd be incriminated as well. I can't fucking believe you." She pushes her drink away and sits back in her chair. "Look, I've had to sit on crap. Shit, I've probably got more garbage locked in the vault than you with all your battle scars. You don't have to worry about me. I told you I was in this for Tiffany. As far as I'm concerned, you're the Angel of Justice."

I exhale and polish off my scotch. "There's no such thing."

Toni shakes her head and stands. "I'm taking off. You don't have to worry about me. I think you did the right thing. The *only* thing."

Patrick calls after her. "I'll check in with you in a few days."

She keeps walking, and we sit for a moment in silence then I look up at my partner. "We're finished here."

He tips his glass and kills his vodka. "Fuckin A. I don't think I've ever wanted to see Elaine this bad since I've known her."

Remembering my tension all those weeks ago and how good it felt to find Melissa waiting for me in my condo, I know he's right. The best thing to soothe this pain away are her sweet arms, the reason I'm here.

My love.

Chapter 14: What Needs to Be Done
Melissa

Warmth surges all around my body, and that fresh, faintly woodsy scent I love touches my nose. Pressing my cheek into my pillow, I'm so in love with this dream, I don't want to wake up. It's so vivid, and I miss him so much.

At last, after hours of tossing and turning all night, being restless and worried, tension gripping my shoulders, not knowing if I'll sleep again... my whole body is relaxed. I'm so cozy, I want to stay here all day in this lovely fantasy of having him in my bed.

If only the morning light weren't pressing against my eyelids. If only I didn't have to work...

Stretching my arms wide, my eyes fly open when my fist makes contact with a warm, hot body. *It's not a dream!*

"That's some left hook you've got there." Derek's low voice ignites a burst of heat through my chest, down to my toes, and I dive into his arms. I love the sound of his laughter as he kisses my head

"You're back! When did you get in?" My stomach is on his chest, and I'm holding his face as I kiss his nose, his cheeks, his eyes, his eyebrows.

He rolls us so that I'm on my back beneath him, and he's propped above me, his forearms on each side of my head. "Early this morning." Another (thrilling) little kiss. "Patrick and I agreed—no more hotel beds. We wanted to be with our ladies."

Nodding, I slide my fingers into his dark waves as he peppers my ears, eyes, nose with kisses. "That six-hour drive is a little better than starting in Princeton."

"A lot better. Especially now." He dips his head and covers my mouth with his. The scuff of his beard against my skin is so sexy, it makes me laugh. I turn my cheek and wrap my arms around his neck, holding him close. Soft lips move up to my jaw then to my ear, where he whispers. "I can only think of one thing I like more."

"Hmm…" I play coy. "I wonder what that might be."

His head pops up, and sparkling blue eyes meet mine. "Applewood smoked bacon."

"What!"

He laughs and claims my mouth again, tongues twining, heat flaring between my thighs. I want him so much. My chin pushes up, and I break our kiss. "Seven days is over my limit."

"I agree." His mouth is moving down, following the line of my neck. I'm in a sleep shirt and PJ pants, but that doesn't stop him. Catching my breast through the thin material with his lips, he pulls my nipple, and the effect is excruciating.

"Derek!" I gasp, and in one swift movement, my top is off and his mouth is back on my now-bare breast. He pulls hard again, causing the tip to lengthen, and I'm so wet already. He's got me right on the edge with only his kisses.

"Yes, seven days." My voice is a shaky gasp. "Too long."

Large hands span my belly, and he pulls up, inspecting the size. "Look at you!" He leans down to kiss the swell of our little baby. "How is your luscious mom treating you?" He speaks into my navel, and then he turns and presses his ear against it as if listening.

I can't help a laugh, threading my fingers into his hair again. He looks up at me and smiles, the corners of his eyes lining in the most handsome way.

"You look very happy," I whisper, holding him as his head rests on baby. "More than you have in a while."

He rises back up beside me, resting his cheek on his hand and smoothing my hair off my face. "I feel like a weight's been lifted."

"Is it over?"

My question changes his expression to serious. "We handled the problem. You're safe. It's the only thing I've wanted since that day in October."

I know what day he means—the day I went to his office so angry with him. I'd forced him to look at the evidence against Sloan.

It was an emotional act I've often wished I hadn't committed. I'd filed away what happened to me in my heart, and I hadn't considered how deeply that photo of my battered face would affect him.

"What happened?"

For a moment he doesn't answer me. His eyes travel from mine up to the little scar and back again. "Will you

173

accept for now that we fixed it so he can never hurt you again?"

My lips press together as I think about it. He's here, safe in my arms. My fears over what might happen did not come true. Most of all, he wouldn't tell me things were fixed if they weren't.

I consider all of it and make my decision. "I'll accept that for now." Reaching up, I smooth my hands on his cheeks. "I love you so much."

He leans forward and kisses me, gently at first, growing more forceful. He lifts up slightly and catches my lip between his, giving it a little pull. It sparks the desire that had only paused, and I'm pulling him to me, consuming him in a kiss so desperately hungry, it's never satisfied.

He lets out a low noise and circles his arm around me, lifting and turning me so that my back is to his chest, my ass pressed into his pelvis. I barely have time to note his erection before he catches my thigh, moving it up and to the back slightly, allowing him to fill me with his enormous length from behind.

"Aaah!" My head drops back, and he grasps my clit, massaging as he thrusts into me.

"Oh, god!" I can't stop another cry as his lips touch my neck, his beard scratching across the tops of my shoulders. I shiver at the intense eroticism.

He pushes into me hard as his fingers move nonstop over my sensitive bud. His mouth follows a line down the back of my neck, and sizzling waves of fire shoot down my inner thighs. I'm on the verge of screaming the pleasure is so strong. He doesn't slow, and I'm hurtling toward the edge, eyes closed, only waves of pleasure shimmering through me.

"Come now." His lips are a low vibration at my ear, and I moan. "Come." And with his next thrust, my legs erupt into orgasmic shaking. I cry out, overcome by the powerful wave of ecstasy flashing through me.

My body tries to fold together with the pull of it, but he holds me up, still thrusting as my inner muscles tense and pull. I'm arching back against him moaning, unable to endure much more. He's not far behind, and with a loud groan, he shoots off deep inside me.

Strong arms move from my shoulders around my ribcage, just above the swell of my stomach, and he's holding me tight against him, hips gently rocking. My eyes are still closed as we move together, riding it out, gently slowing as we ease down from the stratosphere. A few more deep breaths, and we both curl forward like two hands closing together in a perfect embrace.

"Seven days." His voice is low beside my ear, and a delicious wave of contentment moves in my torso.

My arms go on top of his, and soft lips touch the side of my neck behind my ear. Another wave moves across me. "I never want us to be apart again."

"I meant it when I said we'd be together permanently after Baltimore."

I scoot forward and roll onto my back to face him. "What will that look like? Will you be here?"

His soft lips press together, and I touch them with my fingertip. I know this is a difficult decision. "What if we split the time for now? We can each stay a week in both locations."

"Will that work for you in Princeton?"

"If we start the week on a Wednesday. It'll work in the short-term, and it'll give Nikki a chance to find another job."

My lips twist then. "I hadn't thought of that. I hate for her to lose a good job."

He exhales a laugh. "Working for me is a good job now?"

"You're a very generous employer. Even if you are a hard-ass."

He laughs, and I snuggle back into his arms smiling. We hold each other a few moments, savoring the afterglow. My entire body is completely relaxed and quiet. I'm in heaven in his embrace with notes of happiness pulsing through me on every heartbeat.

That's when it happens.

I feel the faintest stirring below my navel like a little fish. Or it's more like gas moving in my stomach, which should be embarrassing, but this is different. A second passes, and I feel it again. It's unmistakable this time.

"Derek!" I pull back and grab his hand, pressing it hard against my lower abdomen.

"What?" Concern is etched on his face, and he props up on an elbow watching me.

"Just wait…" I whisper.

We're both quiet, heads tilted as if we'll hear a noise. Then I feel it again, the faintest little nudge.

"Did you feel it?!" I'm practically bouncing in the bed, I'm so happy.

His brow crinkles. "No?"

It doesn't matter. I know it's too small for him to feel anything yet, but I lunge forward, hugging my arms tight around his neck. "I felt him move! I can feel him moving! It's just the faintest flutter, but I know you'll be able to feel it soon."

He hugs me back, pulling me tight against his torso. "I can't wait." I can hear the love in his voice, but when I look again, there's a shadow over his eyes.

"What's wrong?"

I ask, but I already know. I agreed we'd wait to discuss Baltimore, but I can sense what went down had to be pretty major. I'm sure it's on his mind, and I

---

confess, I want to know so badly. At the same time, I kind of don't.

He blinks and whatever it was is gone, hidden behind the shield I know he's learned to cultivate. We've only been together a few months, but already I've learned to hate that barrier that keeps me at a distance, away from what's hurting him.

"Not a thing, darling, I'm excited." Whatever just happened might bother me, but when he smiles at me that way, I melt. "I'm sorry I can't feel him yet. When's your next appointment?"

"Today, actually." I push the side of his hair away from his cheek. "Dr. Mel works around my schedule. Want to tag along?"

"I wouldn't miss it."

The doctor's exam room is warm, and I'm lying on the hard, leather table with my knees bent, turned so I can face Derek. He's sitting at my head, elbow bent on the back of the table, smoothing my hair back.

"Seventeen weeks isn't a particularly exciting visit." I smile up at him, not wanting him to be disappointed.

"You forget. I haven't been to as many of these as you have." His touch is so comforting, I feel like I should've insisted on having him with me every time.

"I've only been coming once a month. You haven't missed much."

Just then Dr. Mel enters the room. She's a bit older than me, with black hair and olive skin, and a personable disposition. We laughed at having the same nickname, even though her first name is Linda. Her last is Melendez, or Mel for short.

"I see you brought Daddy along this time." She smiles, her dark eyes dancing as she shakes his hand. "Nice to see you again."

"I was just saying it's not such an exciting visit." My voice is apologetic, and she snaps to business.

"We can move things up if you'd like. It's early, but we can do the ultrasound, and I need to test for Down's and other abnormalities."

Now I'm sorry I said anything. "Why are you doing that? Do you think something's wrong?"

She pats my arm in her confident way. "Not at all. It's strictly routine. But we do have to draw blood."

My nose wrinkles. "How much?"

"Three vials. We can save that part to the end. Let's get started."

She measures my stomach and takes my blood pressure, checks my hands and feet for swelling, and declares me fit as a fiddle. Then we're off to the ultrasound room. The lights are dim, and Derek is close by my side as we prepare for the scan. We've opted for the 3D imaging, as it's the most likely to show what we're looking for.

"I've warmed the gel, so it shouldn't be uncomfortable." She spreads the clear medium across my belly and presses the probe against my skin.

We're all quiet. I'm holding my breath waiting, and then it appears — his little face all beige on the screen.

"Oh!" My heart floods along with my eyes. His features are blurry, but I'm sure he looks just like Derek. Reaching over, I pull his daddy close. Derek's eyes are shining, and he kisses me gently before turning back to the screen.

"Hang on and let me see what we can see here." Dr. Mel moves the gun lower on my pelvis pushing against my skin and turning it to the side. The image on the screen shifts and wobbles, what looks like bananas pass rapidly in front of us.

"Legs... umbilical cord..." She studies the screen, brow creased, watching. We're all fixed to the sepia-colored show. "Come on, baby..."

We're waiting on the edge of our seats when she finally gets the view she wants. "All right! Here we are. Can you see this area?" She circles the screen with her pen, and we nod. "This is the spot."

The probe moves almost imperceptibly against my skin and the doctor nods. "That's it. Clear as a bell."

Derek and I look at each other, and I hold my breath, waiting for his response. It's not a word. He only catches my face in both hands and covers my mouth with his.

Dr. Mel laughs as our lips part, but just as fast, he's kissing me deeply, again and again, and I can't help laughing, too.

Elaine decided we *had* to celebrate. I didn't tell her the sex—only that we knew, and she insisted on throwing a huge "Privates Unveiling" ceremony at her house. She even invited my mother.

By seven, the four of us are gathered in the Merritt-Knight kitchen raising glasses of sparkling wine in a toast. All except me, of course. I have my own personal bottle of sparkling apple cider.

"Take it easy on that stuff." Patrick teases. "You know you're a lightweight."

"I'll pace myself." I wink as I toss back the glass and wince. It's too sweet, and I'll be switching to ginger ale for my next toast.

"Your mom said to start without her. She'd already scheduled a late appointment when I called her." Elaine's at the stove stirring fast, sautéing vegetables in a wok. We're having her specialty Thai-fusion tonight because it's my favorite.

179

"I'm surprised you're doing all this. I thought you didn't want to know." I pick up a carrot and snap a bite off the end while I watch her work.

"No way! I have to know! How else will I plan the shower?"

"Are you feeling better? About your... situation?" I'd been afraid to say anything about the ultrasound since our sleepover and her big reveal. Of course, then I acknowledged she'd kill me if I stopped giving her my baby news.

"Actually, I am." Her tone switches to controlled problem-solver, a.k.a., normal Lainey. "You were right. One month is way too soon to know anything. It's also possible I was suffering from baby fever, between you and Kenny—"

"Did you say anything to Patrick?" My voice has dropped and I glance toward the living room, where Patrick and Derek seem to be having a serious conversation. They aren't listening to us, and now I'm intensely curious to find out what they are saying. I want to know if it's related to Derek's mood this morning.

"He's been busy wrapping up details from Baltimore, so we haven't communicated much. Outside the bedroom." She winks and lifts the wok, shaking the julienne-sliced vegetables onto a platter. Next in the wok go the long noodles.

I shake my head. "Has he told you anything about what happened?"

She stirs the noodles quickly in the vegetable stock. "He said it would be better not to tell me about it. We're not married yet, so I'm not protected by any statues."

"Lainey!" My voice is a cracked whisper. "That sounds really bad."

She shrugs, continuing to stir. "We knew it wasn't going to be good, right? They had to play dirty to find something to stick to your slimy ex."

Closing my eyes, my chin drops. My brows clutch together. "I hate this so much. I can't help feeling like it's my fault. Derek was an honorable man before he met me, a hero—"

"Hey." My friend catches my chin and lifts my eyes to hers. "You didn't make Sloan hurt you. You didn't send him to prostitutes. This is not your fault. And Derek is honorable. He's so honorable he would never let some criminal get away with hurting you like that."

Pulling my chin away, I turn back to the living room where the guys are still deep in conversation. "I was the one blind enough to marry him."

"He tricked you just like he tricked the rest of us. It's not your fault." She spoons the noodles out on top of the vegetables. "You're lucky you have a wonderful man now. One who won't back down from doing what needs to be done."

No words come to me, so I let it go. "Ready?"

"Help me set the table."

Full stomachs, glasses of wine, we're all in the living room lounging around the fire when my mother joins us. She takes a glass of red and sits on the couch next to Lainey. I'm standing in front of the warm, orange glow with Derek at my side beaming.

"So how shall we do this?" I look from one expectant face to the next.

Lainey pipes up. "How about two fingers it's a girl, one finger it's a boy?"

A quick look up at Derek and he grins, giving me a wink and a little nod.

"Okay... are you ready?" My hands go behind my back, and a huge smile spreads over my face.

"I think my heart is beating too fast." Mom laughs and sets her wine glass on the end table.

"Just fucking tell us, dammit!" Patrick shouts, and then his eyebrows dart up. "Shit, I'm sorry, Mrs. Jones."

"I was thinking that exact same thing, dammit!" Mom's voice is a loud reply, and we all laugh then.

Derek leans close by my head. "On three?" I nod, and he counts.

One...

Two...

... Elaine squeals when he pauses.

Three!

Squeezing my eyes closed, I shoot my hand out in front of me. The whole room explodes with screams, congratulations, shouts, and laughter, and Derek's arms are fast around my waist in a hug.

My arm is straight in front of me, and I'm holding up one finger.

It's a boy.

EPILOGUE
PATRICK

Elaine's hands are pressed against the shelves in front of her, and she rocks her ass in a slow ride, sending my dick even deeper into her tight opening. She's so wet and beautiful. I'm in fucking heaven.

The entire group is waiting back at our place, and she insisted I drive her to the only bakery in Wilmington to get a cake "because she'd had too much wine."

Of course she knows the owner, who said we could help ourselves to the supply closet. Our excuse is needing more blue decorations. I should've known when I saw that wicked gleam in her eye it was a ruse. I didn't expect it to be no panties under the skirt that's now shoved over her backside.

Her ass is so gorgeous and soft. I span my hands over it as she rides my cock, wishing I was flexible enough to lean down and kiss it. Instead, I give her a pinch. She lets out a squeal, and I lean toward her ear.

"Shh…" I whisper, sliding my hands under her shirt to tease her nipples. "He'll hear."

She moans again, rocking faster when the bell on the front door sounds, and loud voices greet each other out front.

"I think we've got another minute." Elaine's voice is thick, and at this point, a minute might be all the control I've got left.

I brace the door shut with my foot, and Elaine bends forward, sending me even deeper inside her.

"Fuck me," I groan, releasing my grip on the door in favor of her hips.

Seven days—you'd think it had been seven years as insatiable as we've been since I got back from Baltimore. We've done it six times, in every room of the house, in the shower… I'd forgotten how fucking shitty being separated was those few weeks we tried it. I don't know how Derek and Mel have kept it up for so long.

God, Elaine is so beautiful riding my cock. She arches up against my chest, and her silky blonde hair spills all around me, surrounding me with the scent of little flowers. I slide my hands under her shirt again to circle my thumbs over her breasts, and we're laughing and groaning at how risky and fucking hot this is.

One of Elaine's long, gorgeous legs props on a shelf, and she groans. "Harder, Patrick…"

"Yes, ma'am." I'm banging as hard and fast as I can, and she moans louder. I cup a hand over her mouth, because dammit, she's too loud. And if she says *harder* once more, I won't be able to wait for her to finish. Her lips part, and my finger slips inside. She gives it a suck, and I almost shoot.

Her body begins to jerk, and I know from experience that's the signal. She's with me, and I can let go, ride this wave of pleasure all the way home. "Oh, god, Patrick, Oh, god!"

Both arms braced on the shelves in front of her, she pushes back, and I finish balls-deep in her hot pussy doing my best not to groan as loud as she's been doing.

"*Fuck.*" My voice is ragged as we collapse together. She's giggling again, and I've got her hugged tight against my chest. One hand's still clutching her breast.

"You're insane." She arches, turning her head to kiss me and shoving her tongue into my mouth. This fucking woman! I spin her around and kiss her good, her back is flat against the shelves now, and she's got both hands on my neck, pulling me closer.

My fingers thread in the length of her hair, and I gently pull down, breaking our kiss. "Damn, I fucking love the shit out of you."

Her green eyes sparkle. "Patrick Knight, you have a way with words."

We both laugh quietly. Elaine covers my mouth, and I hear a loud voice from out front calling our names. The voice gets closer, and we both scramble to put our clothes back in place. It would not do to get caught fucking in the back of the Sugar Plum Bakery in Wilmington. Or hell, maybe it would.

"Are you having trouble finding it?" Franklin, the owner is opening the door and pulling the cord for the light just as we're back to normal. Well, all except for the bright red marks on my fiancée's cheeks and neck where my lack of shaving scuffed her skin.

Yeah, we're pretty much busted, but Franklin pretends not to notice. "Look, here they are." He grabs a box off the shelf right in front of Elaine and then turns, heading back up the hall to the front of the store.

We duck and laugh, stealing another kiss before following him.

"Tell Melissa 'Congratulations from Frank,' okay?" He rings up the bag of blue flowers, blue mini presents, and little blue balloons, and just before he hits *Total*, I grab two "It's a Boy" cigars from a rack by the register.

"These, also."

He nods and adds them to the bag, and in less than five minutes, we're back at the Charger. I unlock Elaine's door and hold it. She starts to get in but instead steps up on the doorframe, putting her slightly taller than me.

"What are you doing?" I laugh, but she wraps one arm around my shoulders. The other hand holds my face.

"Don't you ever leave me again, Patrick Knight." Her lips just brush mine, and dammit if this woman doesn't know how to get me going. "I get too sad. And a little loopy."

I toss the bag in behind her and grab her around the waist, pulling her even closer. "Baby, I hope I never have to leave you again."

She kisses me hard before dropping onto the car seat. "I guess that'll have to do. Now hurry up, or they'll think we're not coming back."

"Hmm… Mel's mom's there. We could take a detour past the beach."

"Don't you want cake?"

My eyes travel from her face down to her gorgeous legs in my car. "I'd much rather have you."

She reaches up, and I lean in for another kiss. "What did I do before I met you?"

"From what I've heard, you almost died of boredom."

"Patrick!" She pushes me back, and I laugh. "Come on!"

Back at the condo, Derek and I leave the ladies inside eating cake, planning showers, and talking nursery themes to step out on the back porch and smoke our stogies.

I can't resist. "So. Another little Alexander Marine on the way."

He shakes his head and looks down at the cherry. "Maybe he'll take after Melissa."

"You mean by being as stubborn as you are?" I inhale, holding the smoke in my mouth before letting it go. "Watch out USMC."

He takes another brief pull. "These aren't too bad."

"They're not too good either."

A short laugh is all I get, and I know he's not okay. From the deflection of a little military son to the shadow covering his smiles all night, I know what's bothering him. I've known it since the night we sat at that little table in the Four Seasons drinking the adrenaline away. As horny as I'd been for Elaine, I'd actually insisted we come back early for him. I've seen it before, guys forgetting why we're doing what we do. He needed to see Melissa.

Rolling the cigar in my fingers, I have an idea. "I'm headed down to Raleigh tomorrow. I need to pay Toni, and I'd planned to give her that other money as well, be sure she's okay."

He still doesn't respond, so I continue. "Heck, if she forgets Baltimore as easily as she forgot the number she pulled on me, we're fine. Want to ride along?"

That catches his attention. "Sure. What time you leaving?"

"Nine?"

He nods. "I'll be ready."

We're quiet again, watching the trees and smoking. I know he's not one to open up, but I'll give it a shot.

"You did the right thing."

He only continues staring out at the woods around us. At some point, he'll have to trust me, and I'm pretty sure after what happened, that point is now.

Plus I'm right.

"According to who." It's not a question, and disgust is clear on his face. "So I'm a fucking vigilante? How can I build a home around that? Dex deserves a better dad."

"Fuck that shit." I'm getting pissed now. "You're the most law-abiding guy I know. What happened was unavoidable. It had to be done, and you know it as well as me. You'll be the best fucking dad to that kid."

"Vigilante justice is not what America is about. We have laws and ways of doing things." He rubs the back of his neck. "I'm over here acting like the guys we fought against. What's worse is I allowed some girl to prostitute herself for it. I stood by and let her take it."

"Goddammit, stop fucking over-thinking it." Tossing the cigar on the brick floor, I grind it out with my boot. "Toni did a job. Just like she did with me. It was all business for her. You want to make it personal. Well, it's not personal. Sloan was a threat to Melissa and your son, and we handled it. Let it go."

It feels quieter after my outburst, and Derek doesn't reply. We're back to looking out at the trees, not speaking. Only now the cicadas have started, so it's not completely silent.

The door slides open, and we both turn at once. It's Melissa, looking ethereal in her thin white top. It's loose to allow her body to grow, and her dark hair hangs in waves over her shoulders. She really does look like a fucking angel.

"Hey." Her voice is soft. "I hate to break up the pow-wow, but I'm getting tired."

Derek's at her side like he's about to carry her to the car if need be. I guess I shouldn't judge him too hard, since I'm probably the same damn way about Elaine.

"I'll pick you up in the morning." I say as they head back inside. He gives me a small nod, and I look back out at the trees. I might be the younger partner, but tonight, I feel years older.

My partner's mood hasn't improved when I pick him up for the drive to Raleigh. He's quiet and brooding, and I can't help wondering if Melissa's noticed the change.

She hadn't seemed concerned when she told him goodbye this morning. The weather's gotten warmer, and she'd followed him out wearing a smile and one of his dress shirts over her bikini.

"Elaine's coming over later, right?" She'd asked me.

I've got to get Derek's head back in the game. Melissa's too cute with her baby belly just starting to extend for him to be so distracted. "Yeah, she was getting ready when I left."

She nods and catches Derek's arm. "You guys don't be gone all day, okay?"

"We'll be back by three." I call to her before climbing in the car.

Derek pulls her close, and I start the engine. Once we're on the road, and he's scrolling on his phone, I test the waters.

"Good night?"

He only nods without looking up.

"Checking on the office?"

That at least makes him speak. "Mel and I decided to split the weeks on Wednesday. We'll head back to Princeton in a few days, then we'll be back next week."

"How long you plan to keep that up?"

He goes back to whatever he's doing. "As long as we need to."

I give him another glance then just say it. "I've been monitoring the police scanner. They found the body."

Derek's eyes cut to me. "I know."

"I figured you were keeping tabs. Looks like it's going just like we'd hoped. The media hasn't been alerted. Company executives are sitting on it."

My partner's mouth forms a straight line. "For now. I'll be curious to see if they can pull it off."

"I bet they do. Reynolds Corp doesn't want that juicy scandal getting out to their shareholders *or* their competitors." My grip on the wheel flexes then relaxes. "You're all good. The police know what he was doing there. That scene had hook-up gone wrong written all over it."

"As long as they don't decide to pursue it."

"They won't. We cleaned it up too well. There's nothing to pursue."

He's quiet again, that darkness back. I know he doesn't want to talk, so I switch on the music and let it fill the space for our drive south.

The woman who greets us at the Skinniflute is not the Toni Durango I'd expected. Instead of being back in her usual biker gear of hotpants, jet-black tease and velvet-red lipstick, she's maintained the light-brown waves. She's wearing a modest dress, and she actually looks somewhat professional, despite her inked-up arms.

"I figured you earned this." I slide the large brown envelope across the table to her. "It's a grand extra. That should give you a boost."

She picks it up, and for a few moments she seems nervous—a first.

"I was thinking…" Her voice is a little higher as opposed to the usual smoky deep. Dark eyes flicker from me to Derek. "I might try going to community college. See if I can be a secretary for real. Or maybe a police dispatcher."

The shift in my partner's demeanor is almost palpable. "Sounds like a good plan."

Satisfaction shines in Toni's face, and I have to blink twice. *Did I miss something?*

"I thought… since I have some experience doing undercover work, I might try working my way into criminal justice. Maybe I can help there."

I'm nodding, wondering how that might play out exactly, but Derek is more than encouraging. "If you need a reference or have questions, let me know. Here's my card."

She takes the thin rectangle, and holds it, staring at it a few moments. "The way you handled that guy… I guess I saw not everybody in this business is perfect. All it takes is having your heart in the right place."

My partner shifts in his chair, and I'm not sure her words have the intended effect.

He clears his throat. "You shouldn't use me as a role model."

Her eyes flash up at him, and I can tell she's confused. "You're saying you did something wrong?"

"Yes. I did."

"I don't know that I agree with you. I was on the receiving end of that guy, and you gave him what he deserved."

Derek shakes his head. "That's not how our country is supposed to work. And if you do go into criminal justice, you'll see why I'm right."

She scoots forward in her seat and reaches across to grab his arm. I lean back and watch this play out.

———

"I know you don't trust me. Hell, why should you? But you're a good man. So you did something questionable. I know why you did it—it was to protect me. And her."

"And what would she say if she knew the whole story?"

"Don't tell her." Toni releases his arm and straightens in her seat. "If you love her, you won't let her take that blame on her shoulders."

His eyes go to hers, and he's frowning. "Blame for what?"

"For being the reason you did it."

The two of them regard each other a few moments in silence. I can tell that statement had an impact, and I'll be damned if Toni doesn't have real potential in some legitimate field. What the fuck it'll be, I don't know, but I'm impressed.

Standing, I drop a few bills on the table. "It's after noon. We'd better take off if we plan to be home by three."

Derek studies her a bit longer. "Good luck to you. You're pretty tough."

"Mata Hari." She stands and follows us to the door.

I stop before leaving and give her a hug. "Thanks, girl."

Derek holds out his hand, and she gives it a shake.

Then she holds it a beat longer. "I won't let my past get me down if you don't."

His lips tighten, and then he nods. "Thanks."

The girls are camped out on the side porch when we get back. They don't see us, and I take the chance to try one last time. "You going to be okay?"

He lets out an exhale and looks out the windshield toward the house, were Melissa and Elaine are sitting on the small couch just inside the breezy anteroom.

"I will be."

"Listen, what you did was wrong, it was illegal, but dammit, somebody had to stop that prick."

"That doesn't make it okay."

Looking toward the place where the girls are sitting, I exhale. "Sometimes it does. It's like when we're in battle and lives are lost. It's for the ultimate good."

He doesn't respond for a few moments, and I think it's possible I finally found the right combination of words to help him see how he can still be a hero.

When he speaks again, his voice is reflective. "At some point, I'm going to have to tell her the whole story."

I take a quarter out of the console and put it on the back of my hand. "Maybe."

Derek watches as I turn the coin slowly over my knuckles, thinking. A few more passes, and I say it. "I think you should give it some time. See if it can go into that place we have to put things like this."

He leans forward and rubs his face with both hands then he looks at his palms a moment. He turns them over and closes his fingers in a fist. "At some point she'll have to know. She'll have to decide if she can forgive me. If she wants to be with someone like me."

"Mel will never turn on you." I can't help a laugh. "She might turn on me. I was supposed to stop you."

He's still contemplative, so I clap his shoulder. "Just do like I said for now. Sleep on it. Give it time. Don't burden her with the worry. Enjoy your wife and son."

That's as far as we get before Melissa sees us and comes bursting through the door. "Derek!" She's running, and her face is beaming. I can't imagine what she's about to say. "I found it! I found it!"

She laughs, and he steps out just in time to catch her as she jumps, spinning them both in her excitement. Elaine follows her and walks around the car to give me a hug. I kiss her head, completely preoccupied by what Melissa's about to say.

Derek holds her waist, and he doesn't seem as bewildered as I'd expect. She pulls her hand from behind her back, and an item I recognize all too well drops down, dangling from her fist.

"Tah daah!" She swings the gold chain with the floating heart in the air then bounces up to catch him around the neck again. "Can you believe it?"

He hugs her back, and I watch his eyes close slowly. "Where was it?"

My brow lines. I fucking know where it was as well as he does — and who had it — but it's clear my partner is working an angle.

Melissa pops back again. "In the cushions of that damn couch! As many times as I tore it apart. I can't believe it was there all the time!"

"I'm so happy." His voice is low, and he puts both hands on the sides of her head, smoothing her hair back with his thumbs. I never got the whole story on why that particular item of jewelry made him snap in Baltimore. I probably never will.

"You guys coming over tonight?" Elaine walks around to her car. "I'll follow Patrick back. I want to shower."

She gives me a little wink, and I'm ready to let Derek and Melissa ride off into the sunset. It's time for Elaine and me to get dirty while getting clean.

"Yes!" Melissa turns to us. Derek's hands are on her shoulders. "Oh, and Patrick?"

I squint back at her. "Yeah?"

"Thank you."

I tip two fingers at my forehead and give her a little salute. "I'm the Guard, baby. Protection is what I do best."

She gives me a smile, and even Derek's expression softens. They're going to be fine. In that moment, I'm confident we all are.

The End.

If you enjoyed this book by this author, please consider leaving a short, sweet review on Amazon, Barnes & Noble, and/or Goodreads!

Reviews help your favorite authors sell more books and reach new readers!

* * *

Never miss a New Release by Tia Louise!
Sign up for the New Release Mailing list today!
(http://eepurl.com/Lcmv1)*
*Please add allnightreads@gmail.com to your contacts so it doesn't bounce to spam.

-Hear the music that inspired the One to Hold series on Spotify! (https://play.spotify.com/user/authortialouise)

-See the images that inspired *One to Protect* on Pinterest! (http://www.pinterest.com/AuthorTiaLouise/one-to-protect)

-Keep up with Derek and Patrick on their Facebook Page: *The Alexander-Knight Files*! (https://www.facebook.com/pages/Alexander-Knight-Files/1446875125542823)

* * *

ACKNOWLEDGMENTS

First, I have to thank *you*, my amazing readers! Who knew in October 2013 I'd write three books in this superfun series with more on the way? Thank you all for the emails and photo teasers and quotes and for just sharing how much you love Derek and Melissa and Patrick and Elaine (and Kenny and all the secondary characters) with me! It means so much, and it is so motivational. I wish I could give you all a big squeeze — please take these virtual hugs!

Thanks to my dear husband, Mr. TL, who is the most amazing partner, the greatest editor, my "chief brainstormer," male POV expert, the butter to my bread... LOL! Love you so much. And to my two little ladies, who keep me giggling and who are so patient with mommy when she's working all the time.

An absolute HUGE Thank You goes to the indispensible Erica Duvall, who I could not do all this without! You're not just a great reader-friend and fan, you're my girl Friday! Love you! Thanks also to Kelley Langlois for getting that ball rolling and for being so sage and encouraging and funny and awesome. You're the best.

I love love LOVE my street team, my "Keepers"! You have all become friends to me, and as much as anybody, you guys are just *amazing* in your support and encouragement and sharing! Thank you so much to Ilona Townsel, Jackie Wright, Rebecca Bennett, Nicole Huffman, Melissa Tholen, Chrissy Fletcher, Karrie Puskas, Heather Carver, Jas Dela Cruz, Christi Curtis, Daphnie Bennett, Lisa Maurer, Teresa Gomez, Jennifer Marr, Melissa Jones, Jennifer Noe, Lisa Gerould, Lorraine Black, Amber Gleisner, Lucinda Pilsbury, Angela

Craney, Holly Leffler, Evette Reads, Becky Barney, Jennifer LaFon, Richelle Robinson, Jess Danowski, Zee Hayat, Brandelyn Harris, Ali Hymer, Jennifer Engel, Autumn Davis, Angie Lynch, Maria Barquero, Laura Goff, Ellen Widom, Katrina Boone, and "honorary members" Nikki Hardie and Christina "Bookalicious" Badder. You guys are so fantastic—you keep me going when I'm tired and you make me feel better when I'm discouraged. Love you all so much!

Another HUGE Thank You goes to my superfly team of beta readers and critique partners, who I adore and who make me shine. Love you, Aleatha Romig, Kate Roth, Tami Johnson, Ginger Sharp ("Princeton expert"), Tracy Womack ("eagle eye"), and Rebecca Bennett ("sticker queen").

So many bloggers have supported me since September 2013 in large and small ways, I don't even know how I can begin to list you all here. It would take pages and pages, and invariably, I'd leave someone out. I will give a special Thanks to Melanie "Sassymum," and Ali and DebbieReadsandBlogs for inviting me to my very first author events—what a thrill! To Angie Lynch for making me a Smut Muffin (LOL!), and to Tamela Gibson for putting Patrick on the banner in The Library (WOW!). Everyone else, please know how much I appreciate all of you. You've been so kind and happy to help, and every time it makes my day. I hope all the best for all of you.

Every one who leaves a happy, encouraging review, sends me a kind word, or simply buys my books and enjoys them, I appreciate you more than I can say.

Thank you! <3

Tia Louise is a former journalist, world-traveler, and collector of beautiful men (who inspire <u>all</u> of her stories. *wink*) — turned wife, mommy, and novelist.

She lives in the center of the U.S.A. with her lovely family and one grumpy cat. There, she dreams up stories she hopes are engaging, hot, and sexy, and that cause readers rethink common public locations.

It's possible she has a slight truffle addiction.

Books by Tia Louise:
One to Hold (Derek & Melissa), 2013
One to Keep (Patrick & Elaine), 2014
One to Protect (Derek & Melissa), 2014
One to Love (Kenny & Mr. X), 2014
One to Leave (Stuart & Nikki), TBD

Amazon Author Page: http://amzn.to/1jm2F2b

Connect with Tia:

Facebook
Twitter (@AuthorTLouise)
Email
Goodreads
Pinterest
Instagram (@AuthorTLouise)
Tumblr
Blog

One to Hold
(Derek & Melissa's story)

WARNING: Mature themes, strong language, and sexual content. Recommended for adult readers (18+) only!

Derek Alexander is a retired Marine, ex-cop, and the top investigator in his field. Melissa Jones is a small-town girl trying to escape her troubled past.

When the two intersect in a bar in Arizona, their sexual chemistry is off the charts. But what is revealed during their "one week stand" only complicates matters.

Because she'll do everything in her power to get away from the past, but he'll do everything he can to hold her.

(Standalone, M/F, HEA)

Now Available on Amazon | Barnes & Noble | iTunes | Google Play | Kobo | ARe
Print copies on Amazon | Createspace

*Keep turning to read an exclusive excerpt from *One to Hold*!

One to Keep
(Patrick & Elaine's story)

WARNING: Mature themes, strong language, and sexual content. Recommended for adult readers (18+) only!

There's a new guy in town...

"Patrick Knight, single, retired Guard-turned private investigator. I was a closer. A deal maker. I looked clients in the eye and told them I'd get their shit done. And I did..."

Patrick doesn't do "nice."
At least, not anymore.

After his fiancée cheats, he follows up with a one-night stand and a disastrous office hook-up. His business partner (Derek Alexander) sends him to the desert to get his head straight--and clean up the mess.

While there, Patrick meets Elaine, and blistering sparks fly, but she's not looking for any guy. Or a long-distance relationship.

Patrick's ready to do anything to keep her, but just when it seems he's changed her mind, the skeletons from his past life start coming back.

(Standalone, M/F, HEA)

Now Available on Amazon | Barnes & Noble | iTunes | Kobo | ARe
Print copies on Amazon | Createspace

One to Hold
By Tia Louise
© TLM Productions, 2013

Chapter 1: A One-Week Stand

In the cool darkness of the semi-crowded bar, I could allow the last year to dissolve into a hazy fog, a far-off memory. Each low thump of bass that disappeared into the dull roar of voices beat it further down. With a little more alcohol, it could even become a dream — something that never occurred in real life. Something that could be brushed aside like a phantom, not a true form. Not a reality that burned shame, low and deep in my stomach.

Bars had become a thing of my past, along with flirtatious passes from unfamiliar men, but sitting alone in this hotel club, hundreds of miles from home, I felt wonderfully liberated. I could be anyone. Any anonymous woman having a drink before bed. I could pretend to be free.

My eyes traveled to the dance-floor where younger women in shiny slip dresses and chunky stilettos twisted and swayed, their smooth blonde or red hair matching their movements. They squeal-laughed when songs they liked came on, and the lines around their eyes disappeared as soon as their cheeks relaxed. They could dance all night and still make it to work tomorrow, eyes sparkling.

A bitter laugh slid from my throat as I stared back into the amber drink I'd ordered. The thought of dancing all night made me tired.

The bartender didn't notice me. I'd stood for almost five minutes trying to get his attention to order this drink, and it was gross. "Seven and seven" was all I could remember from the days when I used to order drinks for myself. It was a popular combination then, but I never liked the flavor. Refreshing citrus dragged down by a heavy undertone of bitter syrup. I took a long pull from the tiny red straw and winced.

I should've gone back to the room with Elaine. My best friend since childhood said what I needed was a trip to the desert. She'd booked us a week at the Cactus Flower Spa in Scottsdale, where we could get massages, sit in steam rooms, soak in mud, and let our tensions melt away with hot-wax pedicures. She said it would break me out of my "funk," as she called it.

I didn't have anything else to do this week.

It was with those sunny thoughts in my head that I saw him. At first I thought it was an accident, my eyes flickering across the square-shaped bar at the same time as his. Blue eyes, strikingly blue because of the way they stood out beneath his dark brow, coupled with collar-length, thick dark hair. He had a beard. I didn't like beards—not even close-trimmed ones like his. He was huge. I could see his muscles from where I sat. His chest strained against the tight, black shirt he wore, and his biceps stretched the sleeves. I preferred smaller men, long and lean model-types.

But he didn't look away. And like a deer caught in headlights, I couldn't either. My breath stilled as my eyes stayed on his, as I waited for him to release me. He would release me. I knew he would. I simply had to wait.

Men in bars were after those baby-faced innocents on the dance floor, not me. They wanted energetic young ones with their tight bodies, high-pitched breasts, and even tighter vaginas. Those were the girls men wanted to fuck. They would scream and moan all night and tell them they were the best ever, the king. I wasn't looking for a king. Still, in the next moment, when the mountain of sex holding my gaze stood and began his slow glide in my direction, all I could think was *maybe...*

I watched as he passed the patrons facing each other, talking and laughing. Some were more animated than others, waving their arms and putting their drinks in peril. They all shone in the yellow lights hidden above, in the recesses of the wooden shelves that held dozens of upside-down glasses in all shapes and sizes. Liquor bottles were arranged on the top shelf. For some reason, though, the lights didn't seem to reach him. Or me. We were in our own secret, shadowy place.

When he rounded the final corner and I could see him in full, my breath caught. My eyes traveled quickly from his broad shoulders to his narrow waist, down his grey pants ending in sleek, black loafers. Just as fast, they were back to his face, and he was in front of me. I'd never been confronted with so much male presence focused on me in my life. He had to be six-two and twice my size.

"Can I buy you a drink?" The low vibration of his voice shot a pleasing charge right between my legs, and my cheeks warmed.

Blinking back to my glass, I poked the half-empty contents with the straw. "I have this," I said, my voice softer and higher in contrast to his.

"But you don't like it." A small smile was on his lips. It made him the slightest bit less intimidating.

"How do you know?"

He leaned against the bar in front of me, bringing his face closer to my level, his body almost touching mine. A faint scent of warm cologne swirled around me, tightening my chest.

"You make a face every time you sip it," he said. "I've been watching you since you walked in with your friend earlier."

My brows drew together. "Why?"

His tongue touched his bottom lip, and my jaw dropped. I quickly closed it, thinking how insane it was the way my body responded to him.

This was not me. I did not fantasize about hooking up with strange men in bars. And a cocky alpha who studied me like I was a frontier landscape he was ready to conquer had never been my type. He probably wanted to tie me up or handcuff me to something. A delicious shiver passed through me at the thought. I put my eyes on my drink.

"Maybe I should introduce myself," he said, holding out a large palm. I stared at it a moment. "Derek."

My eyes lifted to his blue ones, which were still holding me in that intense gaze. He had a small nose and a full mouth. A million pornographic images flooded my brain of that nose nudging into my dark spaces, of that mouth kissing areas long-neglected. That beard scratching the insides of my thighs as I moaned and twisted in white sheets, threading my fingers in his silky hair. I cleared the thickness in my throat, feeling heat everywhere in my body.

"Melissa," I said, placing my noticeably smaller hand in his. His fingers closed over mine, and instead of overwhelming, it felt... right.

"Sweet Melissa," he said with a little grin. The side of his mouth lifting the way it did made me want to kiss him.

"I'm not so sweet," I said, taking my hand back.

"Aren't others supposed to make that judgment?"

His eyes never left me as he motioned to the bartender, who immediately came to us. Apparently it wasn't only the perky blondes who got instant service.

"Two glasses of your best cava," Derek said, giving the boy a quick glance before turning back to me.

"Cava?" I did love the crisp, Spanish sparkling wine. Why I hadn't thought to order that instead of my tan cocktail-disaster? "That's sort of a celebratory drink, isn't it?"

"So let's celebrate."

"Did you get a promotion or something?"

He leaned closer, bringing his eyes to my level. My throat tightened, but I didn't move away. "I met you," he said in that low tone I felt in all the right places.

Two slim glasses were placed in front of us, but I wasn't sure I could lift mine without my hand trembling. Derek picked up both and handed one to me. I took it and carefully sipped, watching as he did the same.

"Are you here on business?" I asked, trying to diffuse the ridiculous amount of sexual tension between us. I considered the possibility I was the only one feeling it.

"Banker's conference this week," he said, taking another, longer drink and then setting the glass back on the bar. His muscles fought against the thin fabric restraining them with every movement.

"You're in banking?" I hated the tremor in my voice. It made me sound like a little girl, when I was striving to be an independent woman. A strong woman who was bigger than her past.

For once, I wanted to forget what happened last year. Let it go and be somebody else. I was out of town, in the desert, in a bar being hit on by a gorgeous stranger. Fate was giving me my chance.

———

"More like upper management," he said, not seeming to notice my distraction. "I'm doing a workshop on international trade and finance tomorrow. You?"

"Spa vacation," I said. "My friend Elaine said it would be a week to change my life. Or at least my outlook."

A little spark hit his eyes, and I bit my lip. Did I just proposition him? Did I want to? It had been a long time since I'd wanted to be close to anyone in that way. Was I brave enough to let him in?

Internally I shook myself. Yes. If that was what I wanted, of course I was. I had always been strong before, and I was still strong. I wouldn't let that be taken from me, too.

"Elaine is who you're here with?" he asked.

I nodded, taking another, longer sip. I allowed my mind to release the past and return to better thoughts, like those of him removing that shirt and setting that massive physique free. My desire to see what was under it grew stronger by the minute.

"Will she worry if you're out late?" he asked looking directly into my eyes.

I barely shook my head No. Elaine wouldn't mind. She might even throw a party if I got laid. My breathing had become shallow, and all rational thought was quickly taking a backseat to desire.

"I have a key to the conference room," he said quietly. "There's a small, outdoor patio just off the side. It's very private."

"Why do you have a key?"

"So I can set up in the morning." With that, he straightened up and placed two bills on the bar beside his drink. "Let me show you the desert sky."

"That sounds like it might be dangerous."

His hand touched my arm. "I'll keep you safe."

Safe. It was a word almost erotic to my ears. My eyes traveled from his waist up his torso to his broad shoulders to his lips, past that perfect nose to his darkening eyes. The temperature in my body rose with my gaze.

"You're not safe," I whispered.

"And you're not sweet." His low voice caused my tongue to press against my teeth. I was dying to kiss him. "I'll only do what you let me."

As he said it, I already believed him. His tone was calm, and his eyes said he wasn't lying. Somewhere in my head, the voice of reason was telling me to slow down, but either the cava or the anticipation of what might happen had me floating up, out of my body as I watched him take the slim glass from my hand and help me off my stool. I followed him from the bar, past the dancing girls, and out the narrow exit. Against everything I knew to be prudent, I was doing this.

Desert heat was still hot. Everyone called it "a dry heat," but it was like opening an oven and getting that first blast right in the face. I'd thought about it when we'd arrived in Arizona earlier today, but now all I was thinking about was the fiery heat blazing through my thighs as Derek held me against the secluded outside wall.

He lifted me as if I weighed no more than a doll, and the hem of my skirt rose all the way up as my legs straddled his waist. His full lips were as soft as they appeared, and they contrasted pleasingly with the scuff of his beard against my skin.

Our mouths opened together, his tongue gently curling with mine, and my hands fumbled to his collar, my fingers threading into his thick hair. Soft and rough forged a fiery trail from my cheek down my jaw to my neck. Little moans rose in my throat with every kiss, and I gasped as my hazy eyes opened to the black sky behind him dotted with thousands of stars. It was a gorgeous view, but I didn't linger on it. The outside patio was secluded — we were completely alone — and my attention was focused on the progress of his mouth as he explored every part of my neck and shoulders with his lips and tongue.

He unzipped the back of my dress, allowing the sleeves to fall down around my elbows as his mouth covered the swell of my breasts. My nipples tingled for his touch, and the only sounds were my rapid panting punctuated by little noises of pleasure. Electricity flew through my body, warming the space between my legs, and I was surrounded by the woodsy scent of his cologne mingled with the growing smell of sex.

His mouth returned to mine, and my fingers dug into his flesh. He was firm and tight, and the way he rocked me against the wall, the swell in his jeans massaging my clit, had me on the brink of orgasm. I wanted him inside me. Desperately.

"Take off your shirt." My voice was a hoarse whisper I didn't recognize. It sounded almost animal.

He lowered me to the ground, his blue eyes now dark navy, as he quickly grabbed the back of his shirt and whipped it over his head. Energy flooded my core then surged low into my pelvis. His smooth skin was the color of coffee with cream, and a whisper of hair covered the top of his chest. I reached out to run my fingers slowly down the cut, muscular lines on his stomach, and he shuddered slightly before catching my hips and pulling me up against him again.

My legs went back around his waist. I was still in my black push-up bra, but I wanted everything off. I wanted my bare breasts pressed against that gorgeous chest. I quickly reached around and unhooked it, slipping my arms from the straps as his mouth covered one hard nipple. Low noises came from his throat as he kissed and gently bit. It was a tense, almost primitive demand, his hands tightening their hold on my ass. A trembling moan ached from my throat. The coarse fabric of the balcony curtain was against my bare back, and his musky scent almost pushed me over the edge.

"I'm clean, but I'll use protection," he said in a rough voice.

It was a foregone conclusion—we were having sex. Only my thong stood between me and what was coming. His mouth traveled back to mine, but I placed my palms lightly on his cheeks, holding his dark eyes for a moment.

"Why me?" I gasped. I had to ask. I wouldn't be me if I didn't.

His hands squeezed my bare bottom. "I love long dark curls and blue eyes."

It was enough. Our mouths crashed together again, and his fingers slid inside me. Two thick digits pressed in and out, exploring what was wet with need. My mouth broke from his and I moaned against his shoulder, gripping his waist with my thighs as his fingers left me and quickly worked below his waist. The sharp metallic clang of a belt buckle was quickly followed by the sound of a wrapper tearing.

I held my breath, my heartbeat, everything. My mouth opened, and he slid into me with a loud groan.

"Oh my god," I gasped. He was huge. I'd never been so full. It was amazing and erotic, and I was about to come. High whimpers gasped from my throat as my orgasm grew stronger, his enormous shaft stretched and massaged every erogenous zone between my legs.

I lay my head back against the wall and let go, savoring the sensation. I was weightless in his arms. He lifted me up and down against him in perfect rhythm, and the tightness in my belly grew stronger. Stronger. More high-pitched whimpers came from me, now joined by his low groans. Every muscle in my body tightened, and then... exploded. He bucked me hard as I cried out loud. My legs shuddered with the intensity of my orgasm.

Two more deep thrusts and he was still, gasping, his face pressed into the crook of my neck. We stayed that way several moments. I didn't want him to pull out. The spasms of my orgasm were still tightening the muscles inside me, and with every movement, residual flickers of delicious energy touched me. I held him with my eyes closed. I'd never been fucked like that in my life. I was actually wondering if I'd ever fucked at all after that.

His hips thrust up slowly, gently, and I whimpered again. "I love that sound," he murmured against my neck. "So fucking hot."

His lips pressed more burning kisses against my shoulder, and my nipples tingled at the light brush of his chest hair. All of my senses were heightened as he wrapped huge arms around my waist in an embrace. Slowly rocking his hips again, I tightened my thighs. My orgasm was still fading, and I pressed my face against his neck. Every time my inner muscles would spasm around his cock he'd give me another, gentle thrust and I'd make a little noise, until at last my body seemed satiated. The trembling subsided, and I could think again.

He lifted me and slid out, lowering me to my shaky legs. "Thank you," he whispered. My forehead rested against his cheek, and I felt almost as if it were a dream.

"Thank you," I repeated, stepping back carefully. I located my bra and put it on before pulling the sleeves of my dress back over my shoulders. I slid the zipper up slowly as I watched him restore his pants, fasten his buckle.

I couldn't take my eyes off him. I'd never done anything like this in my life, and I was at a total loss — what now? Did we shake hands and walk away? We'd already thanked each other, another thing I'd never done — thanked a man for sex. Of course, this guy had completely earned it.

He stopped before putting on his shirt and took a step toward me, blue gaze catching mine. "We'll both be here all week?" he said, and the intoxicating scent of his woodsy cologne flooded my senses.

I nodded, knowing what he was getting at.

"I'll be tied up with meetings and networking during the day," he said. "But every night, I'll go to that bar."

I studied him. A one-night stand was one thing, but a one-week stand? With him? After that? It felt like a recipe for disaster. It was going to be hard enough to move past what just happened between us, but adding five more days on top of it? I might never recover.

"I'll be on some regimen at the spa, I guess," I said, my eyes never leaving his.

He put one palm on the wall beside my face and lowered his. Our mouths were a breath apart. "I hope I'll see you again."

I almost melted on the spot. My eyes blinked slowly. "It's a nice bar. And I like cava."

That small grin lifted the side of his mouth, and he kissed me lightly before straightening up and slipping the shirt back over his head. His hair was now in messy waves, and I wanted to run my fingers through them again. Instead, I stepped into my wedge stacks and took the hand he offered as he led me through the dark room and out the side door. He paused to lock it and then turned to face me.

"Shall I escort you back to your room?" he asked.

I shook my head no. I didn't want him knowing my room number yet, although he could easily ask the front desk for it, I supposed.

"Then *adieu*," he said, lifting my hand and kissing it. "Til tomorrow night."

I watched until he released me, then I turned and walked as steadily as possible to the exit, to the spa side of the resort where we were staying.

* * *

Get *One to Hold* today on Amazon | Barnes & Noble | iTunes | Google Play | Kobo | ARe
Print copies on Amazon | Createspace

Never miss a New Release by Tia Louise!
Sign up for the New Release Mailing list today!
(http://eepurl.com/Lcmv1)*
*Please add allnightreads@gmail.com to your contacts list so it doesn't bounce to spam!

Made in the USA
Lexington, KY
30 October 2014